Unconditional

Look for these titles by
Lauren Dane

Now Available:

Unconditional

Lauren Dane

SAMHAIN
PUBLISHING

Samhain Publishing, Ltd.
11821 Mason Montgomery Road, 4B
Cincinnati, OH 45249
www.samhainpublishing.com

Unconditional
Copyright © 2014 by Lauren Dane
Print ISBN: 978-1-61921-962-5
Digital ISBN: 978-1-61921-653-2

Editing by Anne Scott
Cover by Angela Waters

First Samhain Publishing, Ltd. electronic publication: August 2013
First Samhain Publishing, Ltd. print publication: February 2014

Dedication

For the family who makes my life better every day. Both that of my heart and that of my biology. Your love and support enable me to write about love and support every day.

Chapter One

The sun hadn't finished rising when Michelle's phone rang and jolted her from sleep. One bleary eye opened to look at the clock. Six. She'd only been off shift for three hours after working a nasty domestic-violence case. It wasn't just physical exhaustion, but emotional that burned behind her eyes.

But that was the way of it when you were a cop.

Still, it had better not be her mother or anything less than an emergency. Reaching out, she managed to grab the phone without knocking everything off the bedside table.

"Slattery."

"Michelle? I'm sorry to wake you. It's Kathy. Allie..."

The sound in her best friend's mother's voice, the raw choke of Allie's name, brought Michelle upright immediately, her heart pounding.

"What? Is she all right?"

"She's missing."

This hit close to home, but she managed to get her work hat into place as she pulled out a pad and pen. "Where are you?"

"I'm at her apartment. It's been broken into. There's..." Kathy lowered her voice, "...there's mage energy here. It's wrong. Like they said it would feel."

They being the visiting witches from Clan Owen in Seattle who'd taught them some defensive magicks against the mages who'd been attacking witches across the country.

"I'm getting dressed right now. I'll be there as soon as I can. We'll need to call this in as well. But let me get the magickal stuff dealt with first. We'll find her, Kathy. Sit tight. I'm on my way."

Michelle managed to brush her teeth while pulling her clothes on and brushing her hair up into a quick ponytail before rushing out the door.

She still had her work vehicle so she sped over to Allie's place with the siren and lights on, the windows down to wake up.

She had to think. She had to push aside her fear and worry and focus on the facts. Worry wouldn't find Allie. Skill would.

Allie's place wasn't too very far away, just about a mile, so she arrived within seven minutes of waking up. She jogged past the two main buildings and over to Allie's and up the stairs.

Allie wanted safety. So she'd spent the extra money and chosen well. The neighborhood was quiet and relatively crime-free. Her apartment was on the second floor, and when Michelle got to the top of the stairs, she found Allie's mom Kathy there.

"Thank God you're here."

Michelle hugged her. "I'm going to need you to stay back, okay. I don't want any of your energy to mix with hers."

Some witches from Clan Owen up in Seattle had offered a class on how to read different magickal energies, and Michelle had jumped at the chance. She was really glad for that as she entered the place and used her othersight. There was seeing things, and then there was opening up your senses and seeking to truly understand the energies and signatures all living beings gave off. Learning how to use it had been revelatory to Michelle. Both as a witch and as a cop.

Allie's energy was there—bright and vibrant—as was Michelle's. And then she saw it, the cloudy smudge marking a mage. It was toxic, hanging in the air like oil.

Where the mage energy hung, Allie's vitality had muddied. *Fear.* Michelle's shiver slid into nausea. Her best friend had been terrified of whatever the mage had done. She moved through the apartment, increasingly grateful for those classes. Just a few months before she might have missed all the clues hanging in the air.

She took quick notes about the color and feel of everything. Once she finished up there with the police, she'd give the witches up in Seattle a call to see if they had any advice or information.

That done, she needed to call in to report the crimes. Magick could only help so much. Now it was time for good, old-fashioned cop work. Though she was wary, her boss was pretty anti-shifter. The witches hadn't come out yet to humans, but if this looked like any sort of supernatural anything, he'd close his mind off, and she needed him so she could remain on the case until they brought Allie home.

"Answer their questions and be as helpful as you can. I'll handle the mage part, but the rest will be investigation." She hugged Kathy once more and made the call.

Michelle had to put her human mask on when her brethren came in. She got out of the way and assisted with canvassing neighbors and getting Kathy interviewed on the record.

Allie had been missing for at least four hours. She'd left the hospital where she'd been on the night shift, and that was the last anyone saw of her. Given the dishes in her sink, it was likely Allie had arrived home and eaten and had a cup of tea. It was her after-work ritual. A quick look at the DVR and it appeared she'd caught up on a few of her favorite shows. Allie usually went to bed about two hours after she got home, once she'd eaten and relaxed a while.

Given the folded sleep pants and shirt at the foot of the still-made bed, it looked like she'd been taken about an hour to two hours after she'd gotten home from work.

11

They'd discovered she was missing so much more quickly than it could have been. Michelle tried to hold on to that. On a normal day, no one would have noticed anything until Allie wouldn't have shown up for her shift later that night. A whole day would have passed, clues growing colder.

This was a plus. Michelle needed to keep that in mind to hold back the fear.

When she'd gone next door to speak with the neighbor who'd called Kathy, Michelle had learned the neighbor had heard a scuffle but thought it was the television. She hadn't given it another thought until an hour or so later when the neighbor had left for work and saw Allie's door had been left ajar.

Allie was fastidious and hyperaware of her safety. She'd never have left her door open like that. She even locked up when she went downstairs to check her mail. Knowing it had been out of character, the neighbor called Kathy right away. Another plus. Though Michelle did urge the neighbor to call the police immediately if she came upon something like that again in the future.

After they finished up at the scene, Michelle took Allie's mom home. She made Kathy stay in the car while she did a pass through the house, making sure all was well before she gave the all clear.

She hugged Kathy tight, kissing her cheek. "Everything is fine here. No signs of attempted entry." Worry ate at her along with the need to be doing something. Anything to bring her friend back safely.

"If there are mages around...well maybe you should go stay with friends a while."

"I can't leave while she's out there. What if she calls? What if she shows up needing me and I'm not here? This is her home, Michelle. I need to be here."

Michelle nodded. She'd expected that answer but she had to try anyway. "All right. Why don't you ask someone to stay here with you? Being alone means you're at higher risk." After she spoke with Clan Owen, she needed to contact the local coven to be sure people were told to use extra caution.

But the coven was really just a group of people who got together to barbecue once every few months. That was the extent of their organization as witches, though they had instituted a phone tree after Owen had suggested it a month before.

She stood, looking out the windows of a house she'd spent more time in than her own growing up. The enormity of it all hit her with sudden force. Her hands shook and she balled them into fists.

It was not the time.

She pushed it back, as far away as she could because now was the time to focus. Allie needed her to be smart and strong.

She'd never had the two most important parts of her life cross this way before. But the training she'd received from the clan had made her a better cop and a better witch. She could use both right then.

"You have to find her." Kathy wrung her hands and pulled Michelle out of her little panic attack.

She gently untangled Kathy's hands and took them into her own, squeezing. "You have my word. I will do everything I possibly can to find her."

Michelle didn't promise to save Allie, though she'd do her damndest. Allie was more like her sister than a friend, but Michelle was a realist. She'd seen enough in her time as a cop. Sometimes no matter how hard you worked, no matter how much you wanted it, things still came to a bad end.

"Will you call someone? To stay here?" Allie's dad had died of cancer four years before and Kathy lived alone. But she had friends and family in the area who'd pull together to help.

"You think they'd come for me?"

"From what they say? Yes. They're dangerous and they're using our magick to fill a need. Like a fix. They don't care about anything else. So if they know witches are here and they know they can use Allie to get themselves one more? They will. If you're not alone, you present a less easy target. I'll feel better knowing you're safer."

Kathy sighed, nodding. "I'll call my sister and ask her to stay a while."

"Good. I've got to get moving. I want to hit the ground running."

"You'll keep me updated? And be safe yourself?"

"Yes to both." She hugged Kathy one last time and headed out the door.

She needed privacy for the next call she had to make to Clan Owen. They had a contact number they'd given her to call in reference to any mage activity so she'd start there.

Chapter Two

She double-checked the address before heading inside the building in downtown Portland. Allie had been missing for twenty-four hours now. Each minute that passed, the chances of finding her alive were lower and lower.

The contact at Clan Owen had sent out a call for help. They were feverishly working on several fronts on these disappearances and something else the witch she'd spoken to had only hinted at, but sounded pretty bad. He'd been sorry not to have been able to rush down and assist on the case, but he'd done what he could, which was to hook her up with Others who could help.

Which had worked out because she'd followed a few leads of her own—a blue SUV that had been sighted at the apartment complex with Washington plates had also been seen at two rest stops on I-5 heading north, and when Michelle had gone to them she'd found that same mage energy signature she'd caught at Allie's apartment.

Michelle was on the right track, but the track itself was pretty narrow and faint and she was terrified of fucking up and missing something.

So there she was going through the revolving doors of the Pacific Werewolf Pack headquarters to seek their help with tracking. They had some sort of relationship with the clans now and heaven knew they had better noses than she did and there was the added plus that they knew the area.

She walked through one set of doors where two very large men stopped her. One raised a brow at her. "You're armed." His voice was a rumble she felt over the surface of her skin.

"I'm Michelle Slattery. Roseburg PD. Gage Garrity from Clan Owen sent me here to request some assistance in an investigation. My credentials are in my pocket if you'll allow me to retrieve them?"

Eyebrow appeared to relax a little. "First things first. The weapon needs to be put in the bin. We don't allow anyone in the building armed."

She reached, slowly and totally within view, to remove her weapon from her under-arm holster. She popped the magazine out and made sure the chamber was empty before placing it all in the bin they'd indicated.

"Thank you. Credentials?"

Slowly, so he knew exactly what she was about, she pulled out her badge, handing it to him. He looked it over and turned his gaze and attention back to her, apparently satisfied with her documentation. "I haven't been told about anyone coming in, but I only just started my shift a few minutes ago. What's your business here?"

"I'm investigating the disappearance of a young woman." She looked around and lowered her voice. Wolves were out to the humans, but witches were still debating the whys, whens and hows of revealing their existence. "A witch. I believe she was taken by the mages."

He stood up straighter.

"I'm here to appeal for some help in tracking them. Gage said you had some sort of cooperative agreement thing with them."

"You smell like magick." Eyebrow gave her a once-over, clearly interested in more than the way she smelled. It was more admiring than leering. Novel and, well, nice. She wasn't used to being found attractive in connection with being a witch.

She smiled, blushing. She didn't know a whole lot about shifters, but she did know they had an affinity with witches. It wasn't a blow to her ego, or her libido, to be standing in a lobby bursting with all that earthy magick wolves carried. They were sexy and that they found her sexy? Well that was sexy too.

And interesting. "What does my magick smell like?"

"Always a little vanilla. Like from yellow cake." He paused and then nodded. "Yes, you smell like yellow cake."

"I really like yellow cake."

"Who doesn't?" He grinned. "If you want to hang on a sec, I can call up to see who is available to meet with you."

"Thank you. I appreciate that very much."

She moved to the mini-reception area he'd indicated and checked her messages while he did whatever it was he needed to do.

"Do we have a problem here?"

She froze before turning slowly to face none other than Josh Neelan.

Josh tried not to gape at the witch whose ass he'd just been admiring. But it wasn't her ass that stunned him into long silence as he took her in from the tips of her sensible work boots, up shapely legs, the nip at her waist, the swell of her tits—he remembered those quite well—and into her face.

"*Michelle?*"

She blinked and he scented her blush. His wolf pushed at the human in charge. He'd wanted her back then. More than he should have. Apparently his wolf agreed about wanting her now.

"Josh?"

17

Well now. A hundred years' worth of memories fell down all around him at the sound of his name on her lips.

He sucked in a breath and it was filled with her. And with her magick. Fuck. She was a witch?

"I take it you two know each other?" Shaun, one of his wolves who had the door shift that afternoon, spoke, his brow rising.

"Yes. Michelle and I are both from Roseburg. She used to be a cheerleader." He smiled at *that* memory. Her in tight sweaters and short skirts. Christ.

Shaun looked her over. "Yeah, I can see that."

Josh did not like it one bit that Shaun looked at his Michelle that way. He gave the other wolf a look, but Shaun wasn't cowed.

But the amusement he'd expected to see in her features wasn't there. Just hurt and devastation and most likely *he'd* put it there.

"You're here because you need our help?" He took her upper arm and moved her toward the elevators, keying in his code.

She nodded and disentangled herself from his hold.

"Let's go up to my office to talk." He led her into the elevator and punched his floor number and his code before turning back to her. "Damn, it's really good to see you."

He pulled her into a hug, burying his face in her neck. His entire system went wild at her scent as he dragged it in. Her body felt good against his. He'd thought he'd forgotten her, what it was to have her in his arms. But he'd been so, so wrong.

He pulled back as they arrived on his floor, his wolf displeased that she hadn't relaxed into the embrace.

"This way." He led her through the halls, finding himself having to stop from touching her. His wolf was agitated,

Unconditional

pressing against his human skin, fighting for supremacy because it wanted contact with her.

He was better than this. He shoved the wolf back as he indicated a couch near the windows. "Sit. Do you want something to drink? Are you hungry?"

"Gage Garrity from Clan Owen sent me to ask for your assistance. My best friend was taken from her apartment by mages yesterday. There were signs of a struggle. I followed what little bit of a trail I could find up here. You guys are great trackers. I need your help."

Mages. Great. He poked his head out of his office, speaking to his assistant. "Can you get us some coffee and sandwiches?"

"I don't need to eat. I need to find Allie."

He sat next to her on the couch she perched upon, and she edged away a little, pressing against the arm to keep her distance.

"This is dangerous. More dangerous than you probably know. Of course I'll help. I need the facts first so we can figure out what's happening. You're a witch. You never told me?"

"You weren't around to tell. And I know it's dangerous. That's why I'm so worried."

"I need to explain. About leaving Roseburg, and you."

"Don't bother. That's long past. Very ancient history and all that jazz. You moved on. Looks like to a far better life. I'm not here for that anyway."

He didn't want her to think it was about her. He hated that part. He'd left for his sanity, for the safety and security of those around him. He'd left to step into a new life and he didn't regret that part. Still, it agitated him that she was upset in any way. And she was. She could say all the right words, but he could feel it in the tension of her body, hear it in the tone of her voice. Could scent the acrid burn of her emotions.

"I was bitten my first semester of school. It's...difficult to be changed when you're a nineteen-year-old. I didn't know how to handle it. The wolf who changed me was out of control and his Alpha came to find me. They brought me back to their pack house. It took a year to learn how to handle the wolf. I *couldn't* go back to Roseburg. That part of my life was done. We weren't out then. What was I going to tell you? You were still in high school." He'd had to leave everything and everyone behind. And in the end, it had been the right choice.

She let out a long sigh and he had to force himself not to push.

He changed the subject. "Tell me about your friend. Were the police called? Why are *you* here instead of the local coven people? Why isn't Gage here? You're part of their territory. This is big deal, big bad stuff. You could get hurt. Or worse."

"I *am* the police. I've been a cop for seven years now. And from what I understand, Owen is doing all it can with all the disappearances. Gage sent me here but said to remain in touch and that they'd send help when they could."

Oh.

The food arrived, and he found himself sort of shocked at the bone-deep need to be sure she ate it.

"How did you know it was mages?" He indicated the food. "You should eat. If we're going out tracking, you'll need the energy."

She frowned slightly, but took a bite and then several more.

"I knew it was mages because Owen did these classes, taught the people in our coven how to detect their energy. Once you see it, the mage energy, you can't mistake it for anything else." She shuddered. "Allie—you might remember her—Allison Packer? She's been my best friend since third grade. Her mother got a call from a neighbor. She went over to Allie's place, saw the mess and called me."

"Tell me about what you found at the scene."

"Tell *me* why you're so bossy about it."

He wasn't the only one who'd changed over the years. *This* Michelle was firmly in charge of herself. So sexy. He shouldn't be thinking about that. But he couldn't stop.

"I'm the Enforcer here. I'm a sort of cop too. These mages are a way bigger issue than you know." He scrubbed his hands over his face, trying to work out how to send her away from the danger.

"You are so not going to convince me to go home like a good little girl."

"You always could read my mind."

She could mainly because he wore his emotions on his face so clearly. Not so much now, but she knew, given the way he was talking, that he figured he could take over and send her away and that was *not* going to happen. He was obviously used to being obeyed. Ha. He'd better buckle up because she wasn't the blind-obedience type.

"So stop dicking me around and tell me what is going on."

"This is bad, Michelle."

"Give me details. Help me. Help me find her, damn it."

He blew out a breath.

Josh had been a big guy in school. Broad shouldered. His honey blond hair had been very short then. But not now. It reached his shoulders and matched the neat goatee he wore. He was sun-kissed. Which only highlighted the pale green eyes. He was still big, but now he was a man.

Ha. A man. He was a freaking *werewolf.* God.

He smelled good. Wore some seriously well-fitting and expensive clothes. Given the size of his office and the view it came with, Josh was *someone* within Pacific. That and the respect she'd seen him given.

Gone was the genial, laid-back football player she'd loved so hard when she was young. He was bossy now. Way bossier than he had been then. She was around bossy men all day, most cops tended to be alpha personalities. She dealt with it, knew how to handle them, how to push back when it was necessary. She was an alpha too after all.

But Josh? He emanated that energy that only his kind of alpha male had. Charismatic. Powerful. He commanded attention simply with his presence.

Josh the man made her tingly in ways she couldn't have even begun to dream about when she was sixteen. Still, she wasn't going to be managed or handled, even by a man as searingly sexy as the one next to her was.

"I can scent it, you know." His voice had gone low, stroking over her senses like a caress.

"Huh?" She knew she blushed.

"Arousal." He leaned in very close, and she told herself—quite sternly—to get up and move out of his reach. And sat right where she was, fascinated by the way his nostrils flared a little and his eyes had gone an otherworldly shade of green. "I can scent the rush of blood to your skin in your blush. The way you just got all wet." He paused, breathing deep again, and she nearly moaned. She should be horrified, but that was *not* what was happening at all.

She swallowed the moan back. "I'm in charge of my parts. Tell me about what's going on." Her voice was breathy, so not authoritative.

He smiled. A slight tip upward at the corner of his mouth where his dimple showed. She wanted to lick it. The moment stretched between them in a way she couldn't find the energy to disentangle herself from.

Allie.

She sat back, getting some distance, and his hand shot out, far quicker than she'd anticipated, latching on to her knee. She gulped, her heart thundering as she licked her lips.

"*Allie*," she said out loud, and he nodded, but kept his hand on her knee.

"The mages have been working with turned witches. In an increasingly organized fashion. All across the country—hell, Canada too—witches have gone missing, only to be found a few days later." He shut up and she shook her head.

"I *need* to know the details. I'm a cop, Josh. I can't find her...I can't protect my people if I don't know what's going on."

"They're found dead. Totally drained. The numbers have been increasing and they've recently begun kidnapping Weres too."

She knew she'd paled, could feel the blood rush away from her face as shock smacked her. "Good God."

"Yes. Since you've spoken with Gage, you know we've got some contacts with them and Clan Gennessee to the south. The witches are aware and working on a unified defense. Back east where this all first started, we've created a coordinated effort with the de La Vega Jamboree. Jaguar shifters," he added when she looked confused. "And of course with National. That's the sort of united governing pack for all wolves in the United States. Anyway, Cascadia, that's the big pack in Seattle, they've recently lost two of their wolves. The cats have had similar losses in the major cities. We've had some stalking, but so far our people have been safe. We think they might be working with human anti-Other hate groups."

"Are you fucking kidding me?"

He started and then laughed. "Grown-up, gorgeous woman and she's got a potty mouth? Be still my heart."

She sniffed in his direction. "If anything deserved all the big bad cuss words, Josh, it's this. How long? I mean, I know the longer we don't find her, the lower our chances are that she's alive. But tell me what the odds are."

He swallowed hard and she knew he did not want to say anything.

"The longest case that I know of was five days. And when they found her, she was in very bad shape and spent two weeks in the hospital."

She stood and began to pace. "Well then, we need to get going."

"There's no way I can convince you to stay at your hotel while we track, is there?"

"No. Which would be dumb anyway. I can see the mage energy and you can't. The last place I saw it was at a rest stop in Aurora, Baldock, northbound."

"Are the state police looking for the vehicle?"

She nodded. "I sent out an alert yesterday afternoon. Though I had to do some fancy footwork with just why I knew that particular car was of interest. Can't very well say I followed my othersight up the freeway."

"Witches really need to come out. It's awfully hard to hide what you are in the modern world."

She shrugged. "I'm not in charge of any of that. I only know ten other witches. Well, eleven if you count Gage, and I only know him from one phone call. All those decisions are made far above my pay grade."

He sighed. "Yeah. I get that too. With these disappearances, well I can't see how it can go on much longer. It's come out on your own or get outed."

"Easy for you to say. I guess you're part of that pay grade I'm not in. So? We gonna get on this or what?"

"Step one is to go to that rest stop. You said you saw their energy at two stops?"

"I pulled off at every single one between Roseburg and here. There may be more north of Portland but I wanted to come here first."

"Good idea. Let's go to the first one so I can get a good scent, and we'll head to the second one so I can compare. I just need to stop by my apartment so I can get changed, and we'll get moving."

"Don't you have minions to do this sort of thing?"

He snorted. "Yes. But I don't want to assign this to anyone else."

"Josh, it's just a job." She needed him to know there was nothing beyond this. He'd wrecked her heart already, she wasn't about to give him another shot.

He paused, going very still, the pupils of his eyes nearly swallowing all the green. She sucked in a breath and got pine and loam. "Oh my God, I just smelled your wolf, didn't I? That's so cool."

The flash in his gaze sent a shiver through her, and she had to ball her fists to keep from touching him. Damn it, she had to not be fascinated. *No.* She needed to remember two things. One, he left her life without even a word, and two, her best friend was missing and in grave danger.

"I'll help you, but I have a price."

She rolled her eyes at him. "Are you serious? Never mind." She grabbed her bag. He took her hand and turned her to face him.

"You don't even want to hear my offer?"

Sighing, she gave him the *get on with it* hand sign.

"Dinner. After we go to the rest stops. Let me take you to dinner. Let me get to know you again. Catch up. It's been..."

"*Twelve years.* It's been twelve years. And there's no catching up. That's over."

25

She knew him well enough to understand the set of his shoulders meant the discussion was not closed. But whatever.

"We'll see. Come on. I'm going to have one of my people come along with us so more than one of us has the scent. Then I can send them north." He began to gather his things with one hand while he shoved another sandwich into his face. On most men it would have made her cringe a little. But this one managed to make it look sexy.

Figures.

Why couldn't he have lost all his hair or gotten a huge beer belly? Why did he have to look so damned good?

He escorted her out, his hand at the small of her back. She quickened her pace but he did as well, keeping contact. "Hold up a moment. I need to speak to my people."

She could have suggested she meet him downstairs, but in truth she wanted to see how his operation worked. It wasn't as if she had regular dealings with the werewolf pack structure. Or werewolves at all.

They had a sort of magick too, she noticed as they entered a large room with several desks occupied by large men. Lots of large when it came to werewolves, apparently. They all came to attention when Josh entered the space, gazes straight to him, waiting.

"Who has some open time to help me with a tracking project?"

"I've got some." Tall, dark and gorgeous stood, tipping his chin in Josh's direction.

"Great. Damon, this is Michelle Slattery, she's an old friend and a cop from Roseburg. She's here tracking a missing woman, a witch we think has been taken by mages."

He took her hand, engulfing it in his, and she wasn't a tiny woman by any means. "I'm happy to help however I can."

"Bring GiGi with you. I want everyone working with a partner until we're clear of this mage business."

A tall blonde approached, smiling at Michelle as she thrust a hand in her direction. "Nice to meet you."

"Meet me at my place in forty-five minutes. We'll leave from there."

He spoke quietly with another guy for a bit and then turned back. "Ready?"

Once they got to the elevator she spoke again. "I have a car."

"Why don't I follow you to your hotel and you can drop it off and we can drive together?"

"I don't have a hotel yet. I came straight here. I might go north after we go to those rest stops today. I need to keep moving."

"How long has it been since you've slept?"

"So anyway, why don't I drive and then I can drop you back here when we finish up?"

"Why do you have to resist so hard?"

"What does it matter? My best friend is missing and she could be dead. I can't just fucking sleep and I don't understand why it matters to you anyway."

God. Her voice nearly cracked and he totally heard it. Truth was, she hadn't slept more than those four hours before she'd gone over to Allie's place the day before. She was freaked and exhausted and on edge, and it was all bad business for a cop to get that way.

But what else could she do?

The guys back in Roseburg were on it. Her boss had given her some time to come up and look for Allie, but he'd made it clear there was an official investigation and she was too close to the missing person to be effectively on it.

"I'm driving. You can stay in my guest room. And I care because I care about you. I never stopped caring about you. I left Roseburg behind but it didn't have a thing to do with you."

"I'm not staying in your guest room."

"Where are you parked?"

"I found a street spot about two blocks up."

"I'll drive you to it, and you can follow me to my place and park there."

"You're very bossy," she muttered. It was a good plan, but he was so pushy about it.

"Yeah, I've heard that a few times."

His car was waiting at the curb because someone had brought it out for him. "Must be nice."

He grinned as he opened her door and she slid in. "It is."

And so of course he lived in some swanky, cool loft-type building a few minutes away from the office. He'd told her to go inside the gate when it opened and to park in spot fourteen so she did. She sat there in the silence for a while.

She needed to hold herself together. To keep her eyes open and not miss anything. It didn't matter that she was tired. That she'd been slapped in the face with one of the worst memories of her life. What mattered was finding Allie.

When all this was over, when Allie was back at home, Michelle could break down. Until then, there simply wasn't time.

He rapped on her window, concern on his features, and she did her best to put her cop face back on as she got out.

Chapter Three

He wanted to hustle her into his bedroom, pull back the blankets and make her sleep. His wolf wanted her to be naked when that happened. The man had to push the wolf back and assure it neither was going to happen any time soon.

A great deal of his agitation smoothed once he'd locked the door behind them and she was safely in his space.

"I'm going to put the kettle on to make some tea to take with us, all right? You probably don't need more caffeine but some tea will warm you up."

She moved to the windows and stared out, her shoulders slumping slightly. He forced himself to get the water on and headed into his bedroom. The need to comfort her built inside as he moved, changing from his suit into more casual clothes. If he had to shift, it'd be a lot easier to shuck jeans and a long-sleeved T-shirt than a button-down shirt and a tie.

She'd grown into a woman worth getting to know. *Damn it.* He knew she wanted him to walk away. Or that she said so. But there was something between them. Flavored with what they'd been to one another before, but certainly it was more now. They were grown-ups now.

His life was radically different than he'd ever imagined growing up in that shithole house with his craptastic parents. It hadn't been hard to walk away from that, not really. What he faced if he'd have stayed there was most likely a dead end where high school would have been the high point of his life.

Like it had been for his own father.

Because of a stupid freak-of-nature moment, Josh had risen in the ranks of Pacific. Now he was a leader. He had nice things. An excellent job. People looked to him for advice. He was strong and fast and feared as well as respected. He'd fought hard for the life he had, and he did not regret leaving Roseburg, and the limited options it had presented him behind.

He didn't even regret that it meant leaving her behind. He couldn't be the man he was now if he hadn't cut all ties. But he did regret hurting her. It had been careless and irresponsible. That he'd been nineteen really wasn't the point.

He could make it up to her. His wolf certainly wanted to. Which was interesting and most likely connected to his former relationship with her.

She was on edge. Frayed. Exhaustion ringed her eyes and he ached to fix it. Ached that most likely Allie was dead, or on her way to dead, and there was probably nothing they could do to save her.

With a sigh he went back out, and she stood at his windows still, her phone in her hand.

"I'm just checking messages. Looks like we have a sighting on the SUV here in the Portland area. So I want to go there first." She rattled off an address.

"That's northwest of downtown. There are some parks and wilderness areas out that way. We run out there sometimes. We'll go there and then back to the rest stops. I want to compare the scents."

She nodded absently. "Yes, good idea. Do you need to be in wolf form? Is that the right term? Form?"

He poured hot water into two travel mugs over the teabags. Just a small amount of black tea with some other things that would probably help.

"Form is fine. I think on it like my skin. Right now I'm wearing my human skin. When I change, my wolf is in charge and I'm wearing my wolf skin. I can get a scent without changing, but if I can shift, my senses are even better. Not always possible in public though. At least not during daylight hours. We'll head over and see what it looks like. GiGi is really good at tracking. She and Damon both. He's mated to a witch, by the way. I think it's good to have him involved."

"I feel like it's my first day of school." She took the travel cup, wrapping her fingers around it. "I don't know anything really, about this world of werewolves and witches and cat shifters."

He brushed a loose tendril of her hair back from her face. "It's all right. I do. We'll figure it out together, okay?"

Her gaze flicked up from where it had been at her feet, locking with his and everything stilled, even his wolf who'd been pacing, urging him to protect her. She swallowed hard and licked her lips.

"I'm so afraid I'm going to fail her."

He sighed, slowly taking her free hand and squeezing. "I will help you in any way I can." She might fail. Not because of anything she did, but this enemy...

His phone buzzed, and he knew Damon and GiGi were waiting downstairs. He wanted to kiss her so badly it was all he could do to step back and grab his keys. "Ready?"

She nodded.

"Drink your tea and I'll be way happier. Think of it as keeping the wolf happy."

"The wolf? Why would it, he, whatever, why would the wolf care?"

He guided her out and then into the elevator. "What I do, who I am now is all about protection. An Enforcer is more than just a cop. It's my job to be sure everyone I'm responsible for is safe and in line."

31

"I'm not a werewolf. I'm responsible for my own self."

The set of her mouth screamed out for him to kiss it softer, to ease the stress lines there. She could think whatever she wanted, but his wolf believed otherwise. And frankly, so did he.

He lifted a hand to Damon, who ambled over and filled him and GiGi in on the newest developments. "We'll go to the address, looks like a gas station, to get a scent."

"I'll do a quick canvass while you guys do that." Michelle slid sunglasses on, and he watched as she pulled her cop around herself like a coat.

They headed over, but it was already three and traffic made it slow going. She sipped her tea and stared out the window.

"When did you become a cop?"

"Seven years now. I was twenty and I'd gotten my BA but I didn't want to live in Eugene and I couldn't see myself in marketing, which is what I got my degree in." She chuckled.

"Twenty and you got your BA?"

"I graduated early from high school and headed off to college. I just ended up taking a really heavy load to stay busy, summer courses too, and I finished early there as well. I was rushing off to do something but once I finished I just didn't know what." She leaned her head back against the seat, and the sun, pale though it was, hit her just right and she seemed to glow.

"I was working as an admin person at city hall, and I started hanging out with a cop." The smile on her face told him hanging out might have been of the naked, horizontal nature. "He was satisfied with his life. He liked his job. He and I had started working out, and I ended up taking the exam because Allie dared me. I did really well and so I got the job, and thank God Mark, my friend, had been working out with me because the physical part was hard. I guess it was meant to be because they had an opening."

"And the friend?" He would hate it if she was with someone. Not that it would necessarily stop him from pursuing her. His wolf wasn't that noble.

"He moved to Seattle. He's engaged to be married next summer. He asked me to move up there with him. But...I'm a witch. It was hard to hide that from him, and I never felt like it was something I could share. I'm not sure how he would have taken it."

"Ah. Why didn't you tell me?"

"I was sixteen when you went away to school. I had planned on telling you when you came back at summer. I believed you loved me in only a way a sixteen-year-old girl can. But I felt like I needed to be sure. I guess it was a good thing I waited. Because you never came back."

He blew out a breath. "I'm sorry. Not that I left. It was the best decision. My parents don't know and they sure as hell wouldn't understand. It took years for me to get my shit together, but once I did, I was something else. It wasn't about you and I was a dick for not at least telling you goodbye."

"We were young. It's over and done with."

The gulf remained between them. But it felt a little smaller.

"It's up here on the left." He indicated the small gas station as he turned into the drive and pulled into a parking space.

"I'll walk with you. Use my othersight to see if I can sense any of the mage energy. Then you let me talk to the people inside, please."

"Will you let me watch if you get rough?"

She snorted as she got out. "Maybe. If you're good."

A breeze sent cold air over her face as she stood, throwing open her othersight and taking in the area. She noted the way the wolves looked, their magick deep green with hints of earth and sunshine.

The paler blues and reds of human energy. The deep azure of witches. She paused, moving closer.

Allie had been here. Michelle's heartbeat picked up as she eased her way around the side of the building, and a wave of nausea hit from the mage energy hanging thick in the air.

"They were here."

Josh stepped in front of her, Damon and GiGi to either side. He wrinkled his nose. "I can scent her magick. Just a hint. Yours is rich and powerful. Hers..."

"She's weak." Michelle tamped her panic down.

"I can scent the difference between the witch magick and the mage. The mage smells like rotting things." Damon's lip curled.

"Stolen magick is perishable," Michelle murmured.

"What do you mean?" Josh stuck close, and she could far more easily sense his dual nature now. His wolf seemed to press against the human skin.

"Witches, Weres—our magick is natural. It comes from what we are. In the case of witches, from the earth, the air, all the energy from natural things. For you I'm told it's the magick of the shift. Of the way you hold your forms. I guess Vampires have it too in their own way. Anyway, it's inborn. We use it, we get more. It's part of us like our blood. Mages steal it, but it's not natural for them. That's why it's magick with a k when it's ours and what they have is magic. Mages use it to feed their own power but it doesn't renew like ours does. So they need more. And the turned witches? Well they're like junkies. They use the stolen magick so often that it eventually burns out their connection to the earth. To their own magick. They have been working with the mages to get a hit of the witches they've been kidnapping. What they steal can't be kept around. It will eventually, for want of a better word, evaporate. That's probably why you smell rotting things."

"I didn't really know all that background. I mean I knew this was happening, but not all the detail."

"There's more detail I'm sure. But I'm a coven witch, we aren't a clan, and we don't really know a whole lot about all the rest of the Others. Gage told me some, and when we got some training from Clan Owen about this stuff, they did a brief history lesson. There's a whole world of information I need to know."

"I'll help however I can."

She caught movement out of the corner of her eye, a guy running out the back door of the convenience store.

"Shit." She took off after him. "Stop! Police, stop and put your hands up," she called.

Adrenaline pumped through her system as her feet hit the pavement. He led her away from the main road and through a stand of trees. In the distance she caught the scent of water.

She heard the pounding of feet behind her. "Don't leave that gas station! I need to know if someone else tries to run away."

Josh pulled next to her, running easily as her lungs began to burn. "Damon and GiGi are keeping watch."

She indicated he head to the right and she'd go left. He nodded and peeled away. She drew on her reserves and sped. Their runner was so close. She ordered him to stop one last time and he ignored her.

Drawing a deep breath, she gathered her strength and her power in the soles of her feet and sprang, leaping forward, grabbing a handful of him and taking him down just as Josh sped out of the trees from the right, his teeth bared in a snarl, eyes narrowed.

The guy beneath her tried to buck her off so she dug her knee into his back and bent his arm up, pinioning his wrist enough that if he continued, he'd break something. He shrieked and stilled.

"God. I don't know why you guys always do this. This is the eventuality. I will get you, and if you make me run, I'm going to be cranky."

"I didn't do anything!"

"I told you to stop. I identified myself. You kept running. Now, back to my earlier point about eventualities." She managed to cuff him before getting to her feet and toeing him to his back. "Hi. I'm Officer Slattery and I'd very much like to ask you some questions."

"I didn't *do* anything!"

"We've covered that. I want to ask you some questions."

"Fuck off, bitch."

Josh growled. Honest to goodness growled and the hair on the back of her neck stood up. The guy on the ground stilled and she got to her haunches.

"That's *officer* bitch to you. Now, what's your name?"

He didn't answer so she patted him down and pulled out his wallet, flipping it open. "Charlie Hixton." She pulled out her phone. She really should have checked in with Portland PD when she arrived in town, but it was too late for that now so she'd go through her own people first and then do the checking in. Easier to apologize than to ask permission.

The dispatcher had her hold on while she ran a check on him.

Very quietly, Josh leaned in and told her they had a contact in the police department and gave her a name.

"You work here at the gas station, Charlie?" She hauled him to his feet and nudged him to walk back.

"Priors. Armed robbery. Reduced sentence because you testified. A few assault raps. Did some time for that." She kept listening as dispatch continued to fill her in. "Car theft. Check forging. You sure do like getting arrested, Charlie. Burglary. Felons aren't supposed to be carrying weapons, and here you are with a handgun and a knife. Tsk tsk."

Damon and GiGi waited, as Josh had said they would, in the parking lot. She instructed dispatch to call Portland PD, giving them the name Josh had told her, and get them out to pick Charlie up. He was in violation of his parole, and if he was in jail, she'd know where he was.

"So, while we wait, you want to answer my questions so I can say you were helpful? Probably knock some time off for you."

"Fine. No I don't work here. I do odd jobs for my brother-in-law. I was visiting Bobby, the owner of this place."

"Why'd you run out the back door and *do not* waste my time telling me you were on your way home and you like running."

"Just stopping by. I looked out the window and saw you get out. You got cop written all over you. I didn't need the hassle. Bobby's a felon too."

A double parole violation with the weapons possession.

"You ever see this woman?" She held out a picture of Allie. He shook his head.

"I'd remember her. I like blondes."

She curled her lip, barely restraining the urge to shake him.

"Know anyone with a blue SUV? Jeep Cherokee."

That he did know. She saw recognition in his features even as he tried to school it. Christ, no wonder he got arrested so many times. He was a dumbass.

"Everyone and their brother has an SUV. Hell you drove up in one."

"Sure I did. But we both know you know exactly which SUV I mean."

"I really don't. I know at least ten people with SUVs. Can't say I notice the colors much."

"I think I need to talk to Bobby about this whole thing." She stepped away, her hand still at his back, and he leapt at her, knocking her down, snarling as he tried to bite her.

Her head cracked against the asphalt so hard she saw stars, and the edges of her vision grayed slightly.

Josh hauled him off and slammed him against the car hard enough she heard the air burst from his lips. "I should gut you for that," he growled low, the words laced with menace enough to bring a little fear even to Michelle.

She got up, embarrassed she'd let him get the jump on her like that. "See, stuff like that just means you're not being helpful and it makes me wonder just what you're so afraid of you'd rather do time than reveal."

"Damon, watch this piece of shit."

The Were glowered and nodded, his gaze never leaving Charlie. "Boss, you smell that?" He said this quietly.

Josh lifted his head, closed his eyes and breathed in. Moments later his nose wrinkled.

"How long?"

"You ran after this piece of shit, and we hung around, out of sight to be sure no one entered or left. When you brought him back and we got a little closer, the wind changed a bit and I got the first whiff."

"Mind sharing?" Michelle gave Josh a look.

"Something smells dead."

She glanced down at Charlie. "Really now? You make something dead, Charlie?"

He shook really hard, and she sighed. They weren't going to get anything from him right then.

Standing straighter, she tipped her chin toward the store.

Josh tried to get ahead of her, and she grabbed the waistband of his jeans, the backs of her fingers brushing against the bare, hot skin of his lower back. It sent little shocks through her, awakening all sorts of things she had to push away.

"Me first," she hissed.

"What? *No.*"

"It's not a request. I'm the cop. You're a civilian. Get back or I won't let you come with me at all."

"You can't stop me." The green in his eyes deepened at the challenge, the air between them nearly crackling.

"I will shoot you. Don't think I won't. This is *my* friend and *my* case."

He sighed. "Fine. Not because I think you'd shoot me."

Whatever. The hair on her arms stood up and she paused again. "Think I know where the something dead is. Stay behind me. I'm going in low."

She pulled her piece out, thumbing off the safety.

Still careful, moving quicker, she pushed the door open, keeping low, and saw the blood even before the smell hit her. And what a smell. Fear and death, evacuated bowels. She kept an eye on the body even as she swept through the small interior and found it empty. She tried to cling to her training, but she'd never in her life seen anything like it.

Bobby had been torn apart. Literally. Pieces of him had been flung about. She took in what she could as she huffed shallow breaths through her mouth and fought the nausea roiling through her system.

Josh touched her gently. "We'll wait outside. Pam, that's the cop who'll come, is one of ours. She'll get a good scent in here, but there's no need for us to breathe this in any longer."

She should gather some evidence, but her kit was in the car anyway. The Portland cops would come, and for the time being she'd secured the scene so she allowed Josh to lead her out.

What if they were going to do that to Allie? What if they *had* done that to Allie? Rage swept through her hot and fast as she headed toward Charlie, who paled at the sight of her. She saw no blood on him, just dirt and some pine needles from when they'd tackled him. His jeans were faded and his T-shirt was pale blue so he couldn't have hid it. And if he'd been part of what had been done inside, there was no way he'd have come out this clean.

"What the fuck? You want to tell me what the hell did that to him?" She pulled out her phone and called her dispatcher to report the body and have that relayed to Portland PD.

"I don't know what you mean."

She stared at him for so long he began to move from one foot to the other. "You got yourself a little hobby, Charlie? Hm? Playing all serial killer? It puts the lotion in the basket?" She quoted *Silence of the Lambs.*

"I didn't do that! You can't hang it on me, no how. I didn't do that."

"Who did, then, Charlie?"

He clamped his lips together and shook his head. But then he whispered, "Listen, lady, you don't want anything to do with them." And said nothing else.

Chapter Four

Pam, the wolf cop, cop wolf, whatever, showed up with two others, also wolves. Michelle hadn't needed to be told because using her othersight she found it rather easy to detect such things by that point.

If she hadn't been searching for her missing best friend and dealing with a dead body that had been torn to bits, she might have had the time to be excited and amazed by all the things she was learning. As it was, she barely held herself together. She'd questioned Charlie again thoroughly and had given a sketch of what had been said to Pam, who'd be her liaison in the police department so that was one less thing to worry about. Sadly there wasn't much to tell. He'd made that creepy comment about not wanting to have anything to do with *them* but had remained silent about anything else. He stuck to his story about running because he was in violation of his parole.

"Let's head down to the rest stops, just so I can see if the scents here are the ones there."

"None of this will be admissible," she mumbled as she headed back to Josh's car.

"Probably not. But we take care of our own problems. It won't need to be admissible. Charlie there is human, as was Bobby. But Allie isn't. I don't care about the mages, as far as I'm concerned they're not human either." Josh paused. "I need to talk to Damon and GiGi. They have the scent from the SUV here. I want them fanning out north and in the area. There's already an alert on the car so we've got that covered. I want to see if the scent is the same down south, but we can split up some labor now."

How far she'd come in less than two days.

Two days ago she'd never have allowed all this non-police interference in a case. Two days ago she'd never have been silent when someone hinted at vigilante justice. Two days ago she believed in the system and maybe she still did, but her hands were tied by the way things were and she couldn't let Allie get killed by real-life monsters because of the system.

What she would do when this was all said and done she honestly didn't know. For the first time in a really long time, she just didn't know. She was alone and drifting, and she had to let that be okay until she found Allie. Then she could go soul searching.

"Is she going to be all right?" Damon tipped his chin toward the car. "Gotta be a lot to take in for her." He did grin for a moment though. "I will say she's a little bad ass. The way she handled Charlie was a sight to behold."

"She's a nice girl from a small town who has just had her entire world turned upside down. So yeah, I think she's a little overwhelmed. She'll deal. She's got a spine of steel to go with her badassery. She made a tackle I'd have admired back in the day."

"I forget you played football. She was a cheerleader I hear."

"Better not let Gina hear you talk like that. Your witch will cut you." GiGi smirked as she referred to Damon's mate, a witch like Michelle, but one who'd grown up within the clan system and was far more versed in the world of the Others.

"Depending on how long she's in town, you guys should come over for dinner or something. Gina would like Michelle, and Michelle could use some allies, people like her."

"One step at a time. Let's just find her friend first. I know this girl, Allie. Grew up with her too. You and GiGi track here in town. Work with Pam on any other sightings of that SUV. We're headed south to those other rest stops. I want to be sure they're the same mages."

He checked in briefly with Pam, but the coroner had shown up and she was far too busy to say much, which was fine. His mind was already on Michelle.

That was a lie.

His mind had never left Michelle. His skin still burned at the small of his back where she'd touched him. Her scent had pushed even the pervasive and horrifying stench of death from his nose.

He wanted her. So much he had to force the need from his mind with other things. He remembered that body in the convenience store. He hoped like hell that wasn't Allie's fate. He'd die before he let it be Michelle's fate.

"Ready?" he asked, sliding into his seat and fastening his seatbelt.

"Yes. I checked in but there's nothing new. Kathy, that's Allie's mom, she's got her sister staying with her and the coven is in touch with Owen. No one else has gone missing, though I find it hard to believe they just stopped off in Roseburg, kidnapped a witch like a cup of coffee on a road trip. This seems far more organized than junkies grabbing a fix."

"Yes. The fact that they're working together with turned witches and have started targeting Weres points in that direction." There was silence for a while and he wanted to fill it. Wanted her voice.

"So, since your cop boyfriend moved away, has there been anyone else?"

"I've been on nights for the last few months. My turn I guess. It's hard enough to date when you're a cop. Your

2

schedule is already sort of wonky as it is, and then once you add night shift, it sort of kills your social life. I work, come home, go to bed, get up, eat, work out, go to work. What about you?"

"I go out here and there, but nothing serious."

"Wolves mate for life right? I mean, that would have to be weird when it comes to dating."

"It's complicated, but yeah. I tend to date only other wolves. It's hard to explain to humans, *hey look, I already know up front this won't be permanent and I could meet that forever person at any point so hey let's keep things light.*"

"All I know is what I hear about in the news or whatever. And it's always so sensationalized it's hard to know what's true and what isn't."

"So ask. I'll tell you."

"You got bit you said. Wolves tell the media all the time that they're safe to be around. Clearly that's not the case."

He treaded carefully here. "That's partially true. I was bitten by a wolf who had really poor control. Most of the time when a human is changed, or when a natural wolf hits maturation, they're guided through it by older, stronger wolves with a great deal of control. But the guy who bit me hadn't told anyone he'd been bitten when he'd been on a camping trip. The day he attacked me had been his very first shift. To their credit, when Pacific heard they came to get us both. Being turned at my age is hard. Being nineteen is hard enough, you're still a teenager, on your way to manhood, all those hormones. It wreaks havoc, and most humans that age who want to be turned are refused until they're at least twenty-five. After I was bitten, I lived in the Pack House for eight months as I worked on my control and I shifted regularly in the company of other wolves. It's not a perfect system. Accidents do happen. But we work as hard as we can to ensure they don't."

"And you didn't hate them? I mean you ended up one of their leaders even after they changed you without your consent?"

"It's complicated."

"Lots of that going around."

He snorted. "Life is complicated, I suppose. But what was I going to do? I wasn't good enough to play professional ball. My grades were okay but nothing spectacular. My parents couldn't have cared less about where I was going or my plans for the future. I had a dead-end in my past but a freak occurrence opened up many doors for my future. I was strong. And fast. I could control my shift early on. Pack life can be pretty disciplined and regimented. I...took to it. I thrived. Each time I challenged for a position and I won, I earned respect. It was a totally different world, but it feels natural to me."

"So you advance by fighting?"

He shrugged. "Sometimes. I ended up as Enforcer without a fight. I was second-in-command to the Enforcer who is now the Alpha. I ascended and no one challenged me. I'd earned the respect of the pack."

"That means a great deal, I imagine."

"Yes." It meant everything.

"I'm glad you have a good life."

"Yeah? Even if I was a dick to you before?"

She snorted. "Even if you were a dick to me before. Why would I wish a horrible life on anyone, much less someone I cared so much about once?"

"Only once?"

"I knew Josh the jock. I don't really know Josh the Enforcer. But I appreciate the help in finding Allie. That's a start."

It was.

They got off the freeway south of the first rest stop and then got back on heading north so he could pull into the northbound one. He caught the scent right away. The mages had a rotting meat stench.

"Their energy is still here, faint, but here."

"I can scent it. It's the same as the convenience store."

"I think there are surveillance cameras here."

"I know just the person to call for that." He pulled out his phone and dialed Nina Warden, who at one time in her life happened to be a pretty notorious hacker. He explained the situation, and she told him she'd get right on it and call him back when she had news.

"I could have gotten a warrant, you know," she muttered when they got back in the car and headed north to the next stop.

"Maybe, sure. Though how you'd have known the SUV stopped here would have been fun to explain, no? *Well, Your Honor, I got out and I just sensed they'd been here.*"

This was a one-way road, and she was far too late in the journey to turn back. He felt for her, knowing it had to be hard. But she couldn't count on human help for this. She had support in the Others, and the sooner she accepted it, the better off she'd be.

Her mouth snapped shut, and she looked out the window as they headed north. The scent was the same at the second rest stop too, and by then it was already dark. He was hungry, and the breakfast bars he'd had in the car weren't enough as they got back to Portland.

He pulled into the parking lot outside one of his favorite barbecue places that also happened to be run by wolves from the pack. A safe space with plenty of variety and heaping helpings.

She looked up at him, weariness all over her. "Why are you stopping?"

"I haven't eaten in hours and neither have you. I need to get a lot more calories than I used to, and you're so tired you're weaving in your seat. Anyway, it's too dark to do anything else right now. This place is really good, and it's run by my people so we're safe."

He got out, and before he could get to her door, she'd managed to grab her bag and join him. "I was on my way to get your door."

"Huh."

He hid a smile as they went inside.

The way they all sort of swallowed him up with pats on the back, hugs and casual touches had been surprising. But she noted the same sort of behavior throughout the small restaurant.

She looked back at the big laminated menu, so hungry it was hard to choose.

"Everything is good. For sides I recommend the baked beans and the macaroni salad. Cornbread comes with the meal too. Oh try the lemonade."

He was really good looking. She stared at the line of his jaw far too long but couldn't seem to stop herself. She was too tired to use her filters. That must have been it. She wondered what he smelled like just behind his jaw, beneath his ear. She'd been surprised when he'd hugged her earlier so she hadn't really gotten much of a sense of how he smelled, though in the car she noted his cologne, and whenever his wolf got very close to the surface, she smelled the forest.

She bet he looked way better naked now. The few times they'd actually done anything back in the day had been rushed but for the night of his senior prom when he'd gotten a hotel room.

She bet he filled out his boxers a lot better. All muscled and tawny. His hair was longer than it had been, he had scruff. Man, she was apparently a sucker for scruff. Who knew? She'd tended toward clean-shaven men in the past but Josh had converted her.

When she forced herself to turn her attention back to her menu, she noted he'd been staring. "What?"

"Whatever were you just thinking about?"

"What I'm going to order. Combo three I think, and I'll take your recommendation for the sides." She continued to stare at the menu to keep from staring at him.

"Remember I can scent your arousal."

He spoke low enough that no one else could hear but her. The place was loud as it was, even if they all were shifters and probably had super hearing.

"It's hunger. I'm hot for ribs."

He laughed but didn't push any further. Even as they ate, he kept it light. And he ate like nothing she'd ever seen before.

"Holy cow, I don't think I've witnessed another person eat that much food at once. Where do you put it all? You probably have like what? Two percent body fat or something criminal like that?"

He paused as he forked up yet another bite of the Boston cream pie he'd been eating and sent her a smile so carnal she might have actually pulsed just south of her belly button. She sucked in a breath, trying to get herself back together. He did something to her. Awakened something she hadn't known had gone dormant until that day.

"You noticed my body-fat content?"

She motioned his way with her fork. "Well for heaven's sake, look at yourself!"

"I like it better that you look at me."

"Hmpf."

He grinned, and God help her, he was so ridiculously beautiful she couldn't help but suck in a breath.

The grin slid off his features replaced by something else entirely. Hunger. He wiped his mouth and leaned forward. "You feel it too."

There was no mistaking what he meant. "I need to find my friend."

"Yes, of course. But you can't do anything about that right now. Come back to my apartment. You can stay with me while you're here."

She shook her head, hard. "Uh-uh. That would be a monumentally bad idea." She bet shifter males were a big ol' unruly handful, and she had limited time and energy. Hell, she'd probably end up getting steamrolled into stuff every time he smiled at her.

"Oh, I disagree. I think it'd be a fabulous idea. You want me, Michelle. As much as I want you. I promise to get you nice and tired so you can sleep."

"You come with all sorts of complications, Josh. I can't right now."

"You still angry with me?"

She sighed. "No. I get it." And really she didn't blame him. It had hurt, but she'd moved on and he did have a better life here. She cared about him enough to be pleased for that. And he'd been nothing but helpful in the search for Allie.

"But?"

"But you're an alpha male and I have too much stuff on my plate to take you on right now. I want to check in to a hotel, take a long shower and then go to sleep." After masturbating most likely because he got her all stirred up.

The check came, and she didn't fail to notice the way the waitress tried to flirt with him. But he didn't engage, all his attention was on her and it flustered her.

"Come on. We'll get you back to my apartment where your car is so you can get your bag. There's a hotel about three blocks from me. Secure. We put people up there when they come in from out of town. Leave your car at my place."

"Why?"

He put an arm around her as he steered her to his car. "If they know you're looking for them, they're going to be on the lookout for your car. If it's in the garage at my building, they won't know you're staying at the hotel down the street."

Which is something she should have thought of.

She grabbed her small overnight bag from her car and he drove her to the hotel where they knew him, and of course everything female seemed to fall over herself to be of any assistance.

"I'm walking you up so don't argue." He spoke, his lips against her temple, and she shivered.

Her scent dug into him with sharp claws. She was turned on, wet for him, her skin heated from a perpetual blush. He couldn't help but stay close enough to breathe it in over and over, dragging her over his tongue, swallowing her in big gulps.

"Fine. Whatever. I just want to sleep so whatever it takes to make you go."

He grinned as he took the keycard from her fingers and opened up, heading in to check the space out and also leave his scent all over as he touched doorknobs, brushed against doorways.

A suspicion had begun to build in his belly over the last hours, and each time he felt the need to do something like mark her space, it got stronger.

"I'll collect you first thing. All right? We'll grab breakfast and head out. We'll go back to the gas station and track on foot from there." He knew Damon and GiGi would have already, but she knew Allie's magick better than anyone else and it added another layer to the search.

And it was all they had right then.

She nodded and he moved to her, intending to hug her, but she looked up at him and there was nothing else to be done but kiss her. He tried to keep it soft and slow but she made a sound, a quiet, needy sound, and he swallowed it down, his tongue sliding between her lips, her taste, God her taste, it rocketed through him, filling him up and crowding everything else out but her.

His wolf pushed at him, wanted to lay her out and feast on her until he was sated. Until they'd eased the stress from her features. The fierce need to protect her made sense, the need to scent her space and draw her close.

She nipped his bottom lip, and he pulled her even closer, the jut of his cock against the softness of her belly. Her nipples were hard, pressing against him, begging to be touched. Licked, bitten.

He wanted to bury his face between her thighs, licking her pussy until she screamed out. Wanted her to ride his cock until he came deep inside her.

Which would be a whole different issue. He didn't have any condoms with him, and the man slapped him back enough to realize he needed to talk with her about what all this meant.

She was tired and worried and scared. Now wasn't the time. No matter how much he wanted it.

Sweet Jesus he tasted good.

Michelle's fingers slid up the wall of his chest and into his hair, pulling him closer as he kissed the sense out of her.

His hands at her hips were hot, firmly holding her in place as she fought not to writhe. His cock was hard at her belly, and she didn't resist sliding against it until he gasped against her mouth.

She was on fire for him. Wanted to be fucked in a way she couldn't remember ever feeling before. He stoked that fire she supposed had always been in her belly for him until it consumed her.

She couldn't think straight, and that's what finally gave her the strength to take a step back.

Chest heaving, he examined her, licking his lips, his eyes had gone that otherworldly green. "I should go."

She nodded. "I can't right now. It's too much. I'm really tired and I just... I'm not thinking straight."

He hugged her one more time but stepped back without trying to kiss her again. "I'll see you tomorrow. Please lock the door behind me. I should tell you one of my men will be on the hotel, keeping watch. You can see us, right?"

"You mean your energy?"

He nodded.

"Yes."

"If you see anyone hanging around without that energy, you call me." He picked her phone up from where she'd put it to charge and added his number. "Mine is here, as is Damon's. You call, do you understand?"

"Yes, of course. I appreciate it. But I'm all right. I'm a cop, I can handle myself."

"I don't doubt that in normal circumstances. But these guys aren't your run-of-the-mill baddie." He slid the pad of his thumb over her cheek. "I'll see you tomorrow, Michelle. But you need to know this thing between us isn't over."

She knew that. And she knew from the look on his face that he had every intention of ending up naked and horizontal with her, and she really couldn't find it in her to be annoyed by that. He respected her wishes and that's what counted.

She walked him to the door and locked up in his wake, using the deadbolt and the slide lock too. A quick run through the room and she'd also made sure the lock on the window was set, as well as the one on the sliding glass doors leading to the balcony.

It was a fourth-floor room on the corner so she was reasonably sure she was as safe as she could be, at least for that night, before she headed into the bathroom with a change of clothes and her weapon.

She stood under the scalding hot water, scrubbing and scrubbing, but it seemed as if she'd never be rid of the stench of that body in the convenience store. Or of the way Allie's face kept superimposing itself over Bobby's.

She'd grown up in a house without a lot of control. Her mother had been all about appearances so she'd chosen Michelle's clothes, what her hair looked like, her classes even. Michelle had been a cheerleader because her mother had been. Her father had been mainly out of the picture, and her mother had gone through men like cars. Trading in for a new one every four or five years.

Michelle had excelled because she was supposed to.

But when she decided to apply to become a cop, things had changed. She'd rejected all that lack of control and had taken the reins in her own life. Being a cop had given her something. Many things. But chief was the strength to take care of herself and others. Physical and mental. She had learned to face her fears and overcome them. People depended on her and that was all right.

And there she stood in a shower stall and her best friend was heaven knew where, in trouble, maybe dead, most likely scared and helpless, and she couldn't do anything and it filled her with misery.

"I'm looking for you, Allie," she whispered as she dried off, going over everything she knew in her head. Tomorrow they'd be on the ground, looking.

She turned out the lights and crawled into bed, the exhaustion sucking her into sleep faster than the panic could stop.

Chapter Five

He knocked on the ornate front doors, smiling as he heard the sound of giggles and a deeper voice and more laughter.

Tracy Warden, his Alpha, his friend and the mate to the two men he saw in the living room wrestling with their daughters, Rose who was two and Lianne who was five.

She grinned. "Look, girls, it's Uncle Josh!"

The girls looked up and squealed, rushing toward him. Josh stepped into the house and scooped them up, one in each arm as they covered his face in sloppy kisses that smelled like vanilla cookies.

"Did you save me any cookies? I've had a long day and I could really use one."

Big green eyes widened as they both nodded enthusiastically.

"Have you eaten?" Tracy asked him as they headed into the living room where Nick and Gabe sat on the couch, feet up. A rush of affection filled Josh for all of them. He loved Tracy, Gabe and Nick. Not just as his Alphas but as friends. As family.

"Yeah, just about an hour ago. I'm still stuffed." He set the girls on their feet.

"I'll put them to bed." She held her hands out and the girls grabbed them. "Looks like Uncle Josh needs to talk to your daddies."

They broke free to give him hugs and kisses and to rush over and give love to their dads too, before heading upstairs with Tracy.

"How goes the situation with the missing witch?" Gabe, one of Pacific's two male Alphas, asked as Josh settled on one of the nearby chairs.

"The cop? Michelle, the one I had a high school thing with?"

They both nodded.

"She's my mate." Once he said it out loud, it was real, he allowed himself to believe it.

Nick snorted a laugh. "No shit?"

"I kept thinking it was that we had something back then, you know? That old spark is certainly still there and we're adults now and she's gorgeous and of course I wanted to fuck her. But I've been feeling more and more protective of her. Getting agitated when anyone looks at her, especially her breasts or her ass. And then I kissed her." He ran his hands through his hair several times, the rush of that kiss still zinged through his system. "Once I got a taste, my wolf wasn't going to let me pretend anymore."

Nick, who'd been his friend for many, many years, raised a brow. "Does she know?"

Josh shook his head. "She's drowning right now. Scared for her friend. And things don't look good, so it's not like she's feeling that way for no reason. She's overwhelmed, and she had no real idea about this world, the Others I mean. So she's trying to manage all that too. I just...if I spring on her that she's my mate, with all the stuff that comes with it, I'm afraid she'll freak out."

Gabe nodded. "Fair enough. But you know this thing you feel is only going to be more and more intense as you're around her. Trust me on that."

Originally it had been Tracy and Nick who'd been mates, and they'd sealed the bond. But mate pairs need a third, an anchor bond, another male who is part of that bond. If one of the mates dies, having that third anchor bond keeps the remaining mate from losing it. But the bond included sex to seal it, much like the original mate bond.

And when that happened, Gabe found himself feeling far more than an anchor to Tracy. And she him. It turned out the three of them were something pretty unique to wolves, a Tri Mate Bond, which meant the three of them shared a bond usually made for two. But for a bit, Gabe was left out, thinking he was in love with a woman he was destined to watch with another male for the rest of their lives, until they figured things out.

God, at some point, he'd have to deal with that himself. Another male having sex with his mate. He knew it logically. It was part of who and what they were, and in the end, it kept her safe. But right at that moment, the reality of it was a little hard to get around.

"Is this what you want? Is *she* what you want? You know if you don't seal the bond, there will be another woman at some point."

"I want her so much I can't think straight. You should see her. Christ. She's so badass. She ran after this guy today and took him out with a leaping tackle. She's fierce and beautiful, and she's my match on so many levels."

Nick grinned. "Yeah? We can always use more badass females in Pacific."

"One step at a time. I have to take it slow. She's not a wolf. Hell, she's a witch but I know more about witches than she does. I want her to see how much more of the world, *her world,* there is."

"And there's the matter of you dumping her."

"Yeah, because I'd forgotten that. Thanks, Nick."

His friend smirked. "Just saying. Did you explain it to her?"

"I did and we talked more about it today. I think she understands. There's chemistry between us, no doubt. She didn't deny it after the kiss. I just have to be smart and take my time. I can do this." And he'd have to use a condom until she was ready to seal the bond, because once he came inside her, that was it. The bond would be formed. They'd end up in bed very soon. There was far too much attraction between them to deny for too long.

Gabe leaned out to grab a handful of popcorn. "I understand why you want to take it slow, but the longer you wait to tell her, the harder it's going to be for her to understand."

"Easy for you guys to say, your mate was a wolf. She knew about this world, about what it all means."

Gabe shrugged. "Doesn't matter. You get what you get. If she's worth it, you'll find a way. You're a smooth dude. I've seen you charm your way into plenty of panties. And you've been with her before. She knows you."

He stayed a few hours more, hearing a report on Nick's niece and nephew who they'd ended up raising after they'd all taken over the pack. They were both in college now, doing great. Tracy came down after she'd put the girls to bed, and they'd watched a movie before he headed back home.

He took a walk to check on the guy watching the hotel, standing for some time gazing at the window to her room.

"Lights went off before nine. No movement since."

"Good. Thanks." He ambled back home, hoping she got some rest because morning would come early and she needed it.

She was awake before six, restless. Wanting to see him. God. God. God. Why did it have to be Josh? Why did he have to be so nice and helpful on top of a heaping spoonful of gorgeous?

And why was it so hard to stop thinking of him? When she'd been with Mark, it hadn't been so intense. She'd loved him and they'd had a healthy sex life and all that jazz. But when he'd gotten the job in Seattle and asked her to move with him, she'd *known* it was a step she wasn't willing to take.

She'd loved him, yes, but it hadn't been enough.

Josh though? Well, she knew him. Or a version of him.

She rolled from bed and pulled on a pair of shorts and a T-shirt. She'd work out in the hotel gym. She'd been lucky to have caught Charlie yesterday. If she hadn't been in shape she might not have. It was a good reminder how important that part of the job was.

Plus, she thought once she got running on the treadmill, it was always a good way to take her mind off things. To just let go and give over to her body.

But of course her body wanted to think about Josh too. She should feel guilty about the kiss, shouldn't she? After all she was supposed to have been entirely focused on Allie, and instead she made out with an ex-boyfriend.

There had been hours upon hours she spent with Josh back in the day. Lying on a blanket looking up at the stars as she poured out her hopes and dreams. When he'd left that had been what she'd missed so much. Being able to have that depth of connection with someone else.

She was close with Allie, but it hadn't ever been the same as those times she'd spent, falling in love with Josh under the stars. Though she supposed not for him either, because she'd been falling for him and he'd just walked away.

Which wasn't entirely fair. Now that she'd heard the whole story, she'd understood. If she had been human, he couldn't have told her. Couldn't have come back to Roseburg to do what? His life was better here in Portland without a doubt.

She'd missed him a great deal. And there'd been this comfort and connection with him the day before. She could talk with him about all the craziness of the case. No one else really but him.

He'd listened. And helped. Had put aside his own job to help with hers. To help not just because it was these dangerous mages, but because she'd asked him to.

At least thinking about him had made the five miles pass relatively easily and quickly. She headed back up to her room to find him standing at the door.

"Is everything all right?" Great, she looked like a sweaty mess.

"I was about to ask you the same. I was worried when I couldn't hear movement inside."

"I'm not that...oh you have super hearing. I forget about that. I need to shower and we can get moving." She unlocked, and he followed her inside, standing very close. But the only thing that bothered her about it was she had to have been smelly.

"You probably don't want to stand so close. I just ran five miles."

He stepped even closer, and she couldn't do anything else but watch, fascinated as he closed his eyes, bent and breathed her in. "You smell delicious. Woman. Magick. Hard work. Your muscles are loose and warm. You still smell of sleep."

She gulped, licking her lips. She knew what else he was going to smell because he'd already told her he could scent her arousal, and she was that all the sudden. Hot. Nipples hard and tingling, her pussy slick.

"Jesus, this is fucking torture." He shook himself a moment and stepped back. "Go get showered or I'm going to do what your body is begging me to."

She blinked at him, mouth opened. She should have been outraged. Denying that claim, but she'd have been a liar and they both would have known it. He wasn't angry. His words were tortured.

She willed herself into the bathroom and showered quickly, turning the water ice cold at the end before she headed back out to him.

"I'm sorry," he said as she entered the room.

"For what?" She checked her weapon before sliding her shoulder harness on. They needed to go back to that gas station. She also needed to check in with Pam at Portland PD to see if they'd received any new info.

He moved to her, tipping her chin up, and all the hard work the cold shower had done fell away as want slammed into her again. "I shouldn't have said that. You didn't deserve it."

Unable to help it, she smiled. "Yeah? You think I'm too fragile to face that I was hot for you and you knew it?"

He groaned. "Why do you do this to me?"

She got serious. "What?" Without meaning to, she reached up to touch his cheek, and he leaned into her palm.

"I want you. A whole lot."

She'd be such a liarpants if she denied she wanted him right back. But there were other things right then to deal with.

"Yes. I want you too. But, Allie. I need to focus on that right now."

He swallowed, and she breathed in deep as he slid an arm around her waist, dipping his head to kiss her. His progress was slow enough that she could have stepped back or stopped things.

As if.

She tipped her head up, pressing herself closer, and when his lips came down on hers, it was like everything sort of clicked into place. He was like the thing in her life she hadn't known she was missing but now she did.

His tongue slid over the curve of her bottom lip, and she opened to him, sucking it inside her mouth. He grunted, pressing his cock against her belly. Her nails dug into his sides, holding him close as his taste filled her.

The hand he had at her back slid down to cup the swell of her ass, hauling her closer. She wanted him to toss her on the bed and fuck her senseless, exhaust her. But they didn't have time for that. Not right then.

He broke away, breath coming fast. "That was...it'll get me through the next hours." His eyes held that light she'd already begun to associate with his wolf. "We should go. Pam is going to meet us for breakfast. I hope you're hungry, this place serves a great breakfast."

"I'm beginning to think all the places you eat serve heaping plates of food."

He slid a hand over that rock-hard belly and grinned like a pirate. "A benefit of shifter metabolism."

She grabbed her stuff and followed him out into the hallway. Damon already stood near the elevator. She waved.

"Morning."

He nodded her way. "Morning, Michelle. Listen," he said as they all took the elevator to the lobby, "my mate, my wife, she's a witch and she wanted me to invite you over when you got a chance. She's excited to meet you and said to tell you there's a sizeable community of witches here in Portland. They're affiliated with Clan Owen."

"Oh. Well...thank you. Thank her, I mean. I don't know how long I'll be around, but I appreciate the invite and I'm always happy to meet other witches. I don't know very many." Her mother pretended she was human. The only other witches she was close to who didn't hide it were Allie and Kathy.

Damon's gaze shifted to Josh quickly before he replied. "I'll tell her. Just let me know. Maybe we can grab a coffee. Or you two can have a drink since Josh and I can't really get drunk."

She smiled. "That must sort of suck."

Josh patted his belly again. "There are other benefits. I'd rather be able to eat like a horse."

She snorted a laugh. "You ate like a horse before you got bit too."

He grinned. "Yeah, but that seventeen-year-old-boy metabolism only lasts so long."

They drove over to a small diner where she ordered a pot of coffee and a stack of pancakes. Damon and Josh of course ordered enough food for four people but the server didn't even bat an eye.

Pam the cop came in right as their food arrived. She asked the server to bring a farmer's breakfast and more coffee, and then she turned to Josh, nodding.

"No further sightings of the SUV north of here. One more west of that gas station. Charlie hasn't been very helpful. He lawyered up right away. Our contact in the coroner's office says the dead guy was human."

"There was magick in the room."

Pam nodded. "Whatever ripped him apart wasn't human, that's for sure. No teeth marks found so at least it's not going to be pinned on Weres. Given the time of death, it couldn't have been a Vampire. I'm not sure what else would have had the power to do that."

"I'm a little freaked that a spell could manage something so horrible and violent." Josh shoved a biscuit and two pieces of bacon in his mouth like a machine.

"To be fair, those aren't witches. That's mage magic. I don't know all of it, but enough to know they don't have the same rede we have. Witches like those in clans like Owen and in the covens hold to a belief system that says we don't use our power to harm anyone except in self-defense."

Her phone rang. "I need to take this." She stood and moved outside, not wanting to be rude. Josh followed, holding his plate.

"I don't want you alone. Take your call."

She rolled her eyes but answered.

"Michelle? I'm Lark Jaansen, I work with Clan Owen. I just wanted to call and check in with you."

"I appreciate that. We don't know much more. It's definitely mages. I caught their energies at two rest stops and then at a gas station here in Portland. We found a dead body there too." She went over all the rest with Lark, asking questions here and there, clearly taking notes.

"I have to deal with a disappearance here, so I can't come down and Gage is on an investigation as well. Normally we'd send someone from our Hunter team but we're...drowning right now. This is...there's a lot of horrible stuff going on, I'm sorry to say. But we have some contacts there in Portland and I'd very much like it if you'd get in touch with them. The support will be helpful. And I hate the thought of you being alone in all this. The wolves are helping, which is good. In fact, this witch is mated to a wolf. But we want you to be supported. I know the missing woman is your friend. That has to be hard. And she's one of ours, as all witches here are. I hate that you have to be on your own."

Somehow it was this last bit that got to her and pushed the tears she'd been trying too hard to bury to the surface. She didn't need that. So she wiped a hand over her eyes and ignored Josh, who perked up when she did it.

She cleared her throat. "I appreciate it. I think I may already know who she is. Damon, one of the wolves, has a mate who's a witch. I got the feeling things were escalating out of control when I last spoke with Gage. I'm sorry. It's not good for any of us. But I'm a cop, I have the tools. And the wolves are helping me so much as well."

"Thank you for understanding. Doesn't make it right, but...well I'm glad you understand. Please do get in contact with the local folks and reach out when and if you need anything. We'll do everything we can." She gave Michelle the name and number of the contact before she hung up.

She stared out over the parking lot and tried to get herself under control again. A kindness shouldn't make her cry, for God's sake.

"How can I help you?" Josh spoke quietly from where he'd perched to keep an eye on her while she made the call.

She shook her head. "You can't. I'm fine. I just need a moment."

He clearly wanted to, but he stayed where he was, which she appreciated more than she could say.

She took a deep breath and tucked her phone into a pocket. "Let's go back inside. I think the contact Lark just gave me is Damon's mate."

He reached out and brushed his thumb over her cheek. "I hate that you're upset. I know you have reason to be. It's not that. I just want to make it better."

She smiled a little and meant it. "That's enough, really."

They went back in, and while she finished her breakfast, she found out the contact was indeed Damon's wife, Gina.

"She said she got a message to call Owen this morning before I left for work. Must have been Lark. You'll like her. Gina, I mean." Damon ducked his head on a very sweet smile.

She didn't know a whole lot about the mate thing. Only that wolves mated for life and had some sort of genetic tie that happened during sex. They seemed protective, but she wasn't entirely sure if it was that all wolves were protective or if it was specific to mates or what.

"If you'd like the help, I'd like to come out to the scene with you," Pam offered as they walked out to the car after they'd finished eating.

"Another set of eyes is really welcome, thanks. I know I'm small town and you have your territory."

Pam waved that away. "I don't care about that. A missing woman is what's important here. And that she's a witch, one of us. You need to hold back with human authorities, and I have to do that from time to time so I can help there too."

They drove out to the gas station, and Pam led them to the parking lot where the SUV had been seen last.

Josh touched her arm to get her attention. "I'm going to shift. Stay right here and I'll be at your side. Do you understand? Don't go anywhere without me."

She snorted. "You know, I've been a cop all these years without a werewolf at my side. I'm not dead yet."

He frowned. "And I aim to keep it that way." He slid a hand up her arm, leaving tingles in his wake. "Things are different now. This enemy is...you could be dead and it's not happening if I have a say and I do."

Was she going to argue? Oh sure he was being bossy, but he was right. This mage stuff was different. And she wanted to see what he looked like as a wolf.

"Fine. Just keep up."

He rolled his eyes and then began to get naked. Pam and Damon had headed off on another trail into the rather large park so it was just her and Josh standing in a thick copse of trees.

She really should be looking away. But hot damn. His upper body was hard and muscled and tawny, like he worked outside a lot. But she remembered. Mmm. He'd always had that olive complexion.

But now those wide shoulders were even wider, drawing down a hairy (but not too hairy) chest to a narrow waist.

He put his shirt, shoes and socks into a backpack.

"I'll carry that for you." She was so proud that her voice sounded reasonably normal given how much her mouth watered as she stared.

He turned, his hands at his zipper, and no matter how many things she yelled at herself, she could *not* tear her gaze away from the vee of skin, and hair, exposed as he stopped halfway down.

"Thanks. I appreciate that."

He didn't wear underwear. Good Lord above. He unzipped and she kept staring.

"You're playing with fire," he said in a low growl.

"Huh?"

He tipped her chin with one finger. "You look at it like that, and I won't be able to finish unzipping without injuring myself."

She blushed, the heat on her neck and cheeks enough to make her glance away.

But he was back, closer this time, and without thinking, she slid her palms up the bare (hot, hard, muscled) skin of his chest. "Forget it. I like you looking at me. I was a dumbass for telling you not to."

He brushed his lips over hers as she wrapped her arms around his body, hands flat against his back.

Wishing things were different.

Wishing they were in her room, or his place, anywhere in private instead of outside with far more important things to do than fuck.

He broke the kiss, stepping back. "Enough of that. For now." He pulled his pants off, and his cock sprang out, hard and ready and wow. She'd had memories of course, but they were wrapped in a veil of taboo. They'd been young. She hadn't known anyone else to compare, and he'd grown.

Considerably.

She turned her attention away, securing the pack, tightening the straps.

"Will you be able to communicate when you're a wolf? I'm sorry if my questions are stupid or offensive." She lifted her shoulders. "I just don't know."

"You're not stupid. They're good questions. And you can't know until you're told. I want you to ask me anything. If I know the answer, or can get it for you, I will. Do you understand?"

She couldn't hide the grin at the corners of her mouth. "It's really hard to concentrate on even a very sweet promise when you're naked. I'm sorry, you're just..." She waved a hand at him.

"Just what?"

He was close again, and despite his nakedness, the heat blasted from him, enveloping her.

She swallowed hard, feeling more than a little like prey. "Magnificent. You're magnificent."

He reduced her to whispers, so she gave them. She was a lot of things, but a liar wasn't one of them. There was something between them, something beyond what they'd once had, past the hurt of their parting. To deny it, to deny what he was there naked, tall, hard and gorgeous and helping her? It would have been cowardly.

His smile was all arrogant male, and it sent a shiver through her. "I'll properly thank you for that. Later. For now? Yes, my wolf can understand you. He can't talk, obviously, but just speak and we'll work it through. He's bossier than I am, my wolf I mean. He's going to steer you where he thinks it's best. Stay close."

He bent and magick washed over her, warm and soft, sun-dappled bark and pine sap. And in the place of the magnificent man, stood a massive and no less magnificent wolf.

Honey gold fur, intelligent blue-green eyes. His paws were the size of canned hams and he reached above her waist.

Before she could stop herself, she'd stretched a hand to touch and then snatched it back. "Sorry!"

The wolf snorted and pressed his body against hers, butting her with his giant head until she gave in and slid her fingers through soft fur, over his head and down his back. She knew that werewolves were larger than regular wolves, but this was beyond anything she could have imagined. Josh's wolf was the most amazing thing she'd ever seen.

"You're beautiful," she whispered.

He turned, his nose, cold and slightly wet, his eyes gazing into hers. She held him, one palm on either side of that massive head.

Just a look, and she felt it to her toes as something passed between them. He jerked his head then, snorting, and she got the feeling that was his wolf telling her to follow him. So she did as he trotted off.

She hiked for several hours with him leading. He sniffed a lot of stuff. Growled here and there as he changed direction. He made her sit, and she ate a protein bar and drank some water while he disappeared for about twenty minutes. She'd needed the rest but had no idea what he'd done while he'd been gone. Probably ate a rabbit or peed or something.

Though it wouldn't do for her to think of him as a dog, it still amused her. She checked her messages. No new leads. No new sightings of the SUV either. Nothing. She was thoroughly disheartened by the time he trotted back to where she was.

She stood and shouldered the pack again, and he growled.

"What? Do you need something out of the pack? Water maybe? Food? No, I don't guess you'd be eating Luna bars as a nine-foot-high wolf beast."

He continued to examine her, sniffing the air.

"Is there something for me to worry about? God, Josh I feel like I'm in an episode of *Lassie*. Did Timmy fall down the well?" That did make her laugh but he snorted again.

Then that rush of magick, and he stood up, naked as the day he was born. And still beautiful.

"*Lassie?*"

"Uh."

He shook his head with a wry grin. "The pack? Unless you want me to stay naked? Though if hikers came around, they might not think it was so great."

"Oh!" She handed over the backpack. "Only if they were insane. I mean, there's water in there."

"I had some."

He got dressed quickly.

"What were you growling at me for?"

"You're upset. My wolf likes it even less than the man does. He wants to carry you off deep in a forest and keep you there until you're happy."

Oddly touched, she smiled. "Did you find anything?"

They began to walk, she guessed back to the parking lot.

"I found a trail a few times. But you did your magick, right?"

His wolf had stopped and sniffed, pressing his body into hers a few times. She'd already been using her othersight, and there had been a faint trace of mage magic, but nothing of Allie. She explained that to him.

"Yeah I thought so. I followed it until it died out. I didn't scent any other witch but you though. Back to your upset."

"I checked my messages. Nothing new. We're at a dead end."

He sighed. "We'll keep looking. We aren't giving up, Michelle."

"I just...I want to help her."

He stopped and turned to her. "You *are*. You're here looking for her every waking moment. You're doing all you can. Let's connect with Pam and Damon, see what they've found."

They headed back to the lot after he'd made a call to meet up with the other two.

Damon shook his head when they came out of the woods. "Nothing. We fanned out, checked near the waterways, the paths, everywhere. Nothing."

She exhaled, disappointed. "Thanks anyway. I appreciate your help more than I can say."

Josh turned to Damon. "Go back to the office and check in. Let them know I'll be home if they need me." Then to Pam. "Appreciate the help. Keep me updated."

She nodded and said her goodbye to Michelle before she got in her car and drove away with Damon.

He moved to the car and opened her door. Deflated, she slid inside.

He got in, and once they'd gotten back on the road again, he spoke quietly. "Come back to my place for a while at least. Please? There's nothing to do right now. You're run down. You need some rest and I'd like to pamper you a little. I'm a good cook. Let me make you dinner."

"I..." She closed her mouth. What was she arguing for? The longer she spent with him, the more she wanted him. More than that, she didn't want to be alone. She wanted to be with someone who knew her, all of her, and wanted to be around her anyway. She was too tired to be lonely that night. "Okay."

He relaxed. "Good."

Chapter Six

She checked her phone every few minutes until he finally put a hand on hers. "Your phone is on. You'll hear it if you get a message or a call. My people all know where to reach me too."

He'd called Damon and his mate, Gina, to come over for a bit. Josh had wanted to hold her. To kiss her and fuck her senseless to wipe the worry off her features for at least a little while. But he forced himself to be patient.

Nina called to report she'd hacked the cameras at the rest stops and that they'd stopped working for fifteen minutes at the first stop and six minutes at the second. Michelle figured it was a spell of some sort, but at least they could work out a rudimentary timeline based on that information.

But it was pretty close to what she'd already figured out, so she took some notes and ended up staring out the window again.

The loneliness seemed to flow from her in waves. He could fix that. Or try anyway. Gina was awesome. Funny, warm and totally accustomed to being surrounded by Others. She was exactly the kind of person who'd extend friendship. And clearly Michelle needed it. He wanted her to understand it was possible to live in a vibrant community of likeminded Others. Sure she couldn't announce that witches existed to the world, but she didn't always have to hide it either.

Damon and Gina arrived, and as he'd figured, Gina was warm, holding her hands out to Michelle.

"You're Michelle. I'm so happy to meet you. I brought cake. I'm sure he'll make you a lovely dinner, but he won't have cake and one needs cake."

"It's the rules." Michelle nodded with a smile.

Damon watched his woman, affection clear on his features, before he turned to Josh and thrust bags at him. "She wasn't kidding. Dips and chips and cake. Oh and beer."

Josh happily took in the way Gina drew Michelle out, chatting with her about every day things as well as magick and witches.

"Thanks for coming over." Josh told Damon this as he poured chips into a bowl and Damon opened the dips.

"Gina would have barged in anyway. I filled her in…a little so don't get that look." Damon said it low enough that only another wolf would have heard. "It's not a secret to anyone with eyes, Josh. Looking at a beautiful woman is one thing. Looking at *your* beautiful woman is another."

Josh smiled. His. Yeah. "I'm taking things slow. She doesn't know so keep your mouth shut about it."

Damon grinned. "I like seeing you this way. All flaily and out of your element."

"*Flaily?* I'm not flaily."

"Ha. You are. And it's good for you."

Laughing, Michelle looked across the living room to where he stood with Damon in the kitchen. He held up the tray of food and she smiled.

They joined the women, and he settled in next to her on the couch. "Dinner is in the oven."

"I was just inviting Michelle to our weekly get-togethers. The Owen witches who live down here, that is. They're usually at our house, so you know they'll be well guarded by a big, badass grumpy werewolf."

If Michelle was there, Josh would be there too.

"I don't know how long I'll be around. I mean, once I find Allie she'll need me in Roseburg. I have a job there."

Gina's gaze cut to Josh quickly and then back. Did *everyone* on the planet know Michelle was his mate or what? "I get that. I hope you'll reconsider maybe settling up here. Once you get Allie back and safe. And in the mean time, you can drive up, right?"

Michelle nodded but her happiness had ebbed a little.

His life was in Portland. But she was to be part of that life. The center of it, of course. He couldn't protect her if she lived in Roseburg. They needed to talk in-depth about all of this stuff. There was a lot to discuss. She was under a great deal of pressure, and he didn't want to add to that stress.

So he'd take it baby step by baby step.

Gina and Damon stayed for dinner and cake and left shortly after that. It had been a really good several hours, and Michelle seemed lighter once he'd closed his door.

"I know today's been a long one. Yesterday and the day before too. Did you know I have a giant soaking tub? It's a good place to relax a while."

One corner of her mouth quirked up. "Is that an invitation?"

He moved closer, his body brushing hers. "Do you want it to be?"

She took a deep breath, her eyes closing for long moments before she opened and snagged his gaze again. "I..." She licked her lips and he bent to do the same. She exhaled, and he pulled it into his lungs, heady with desire.

"We've known each other a long time, Michelle. That means something to me. More than what we were back in high school.

You're my friend. You can tell me anything. I am here for you, not just for this situation, but afterward too."

She nodded, her eyes still on his, intent. "I want you," she murmured, and he drew even closer, their bodies touching, heat spilling between them.

"Thank God. I want you so much my hands would be shaking if I wasn't keeping them on your hips. But I know you're going through a lot of stuff right now. I can wait."

"Help me forget. Just for a little while at least."

He swallowed and had a stern inner dialogue with his wolf. The wolf wanted to rut and claim and comfort. The man knew she needed the rutting and the comforting but the claiming had to wait.

He kissed each eyelid as he did this. Across her brow, delighting in the way the furrows smoothed.

Her hands slid up his chest, leaving heat in their wake. Funny thing, given that he was the shifter and his body temperature was higher than hers. But chemistry made it that way. Clicked with his and made it uniquely *theirs.*

Argument settled—for the time being, his wolf waited for the chance to do things his way—Josh eased her down the hallway toward his bathroom.

She pulled her hair from the ponytail and shook it free. She'd taken her shoes off earlier, and he looked up as her hands went to her pants button.

"Don't undress yet." He turned on the taps after plugging the drain.

She smiled at him. "Should I go in fully dressed?"

He laughed, straightening. "No, I want to undress you myself."

He pulled her shirt and the tank under it over her head. He kissed her shoulder as he slid the bra strap down. That's when he saw the bloom of color on her side and paused. "What is that?"

The way she started and then was very still for long moments made him realize he'd probably growled it instead of asking. The price of dallying with a wolf, he supposed. He caressed her hip, and she relaxed a little as she turned to look down.

"Those of us who aren't shifters have to deal with bruises on the job from time to time." Her lips curved, amusement on her features. "I hit that asshole pretty hard yesterday when I took him down."

If Charlie hadn't been in jail, Josh would have hunted him down and killed him for leaving a mark on his woman.

"I get bruises too. But they heal fast."

He dropped to his knees before her, pressing a kiss softly over the bruised skin at her side, then on her belly, moving lower as he undid her pants, sliding them down her hips and legs, taking her socks with her.

Her toenails were painted bright pink. Her legs were toned and strong. Not long, she was pretty petite, but she was in shape. Powerful. He liked that.

He pressed his face to the front of the panties she wore. Pink, like the nails. Damn. Her fingers slid into his hair, pulling just a little. He took a breath scented with her. With her desire. It clawed at him, holding him tighter than her fingers ever could.

Deftly, he yanked the panties down, and she put a hand on his shoulder to step free. He looked up the line of her body to find her staring down at him, her lips parted, her pupils huge.

If he'd had any questions about how much she wanted him, the way she smelled, the way she looked, the heat coming off her skin all combined like a fist, guiding him to his feet to remove her bra and leave her there totally naked.

"Christ, you're beautiful."

She blushed, and he moaned, leaning down to breathe her in again.

"You like to sniff me." Amusement was clear in her voice. "Also, it's not like you haven't seen it all before. And when it was in better shape."

He scoffed at that.

"When you blush it heats your skin, and you smell really, really good. As far as better? *No.* Younger? Yes. But your tits are far nicer now. Your ass is higher, tighter. Your legs are more toned. There's also the added bonus that we can fuck all night long in my apartment if we want and no one is going to come home to discover us."

She laughed, pulling his shirt up and off, caressing all of him she could reach.

"You're one to talk about beautiful." She pressed a kiss on his chest, over his heart, her hands skimming across his back, helping to shove his pants down before she took handfuls of his ass and hauled him close.

So good. Skin to skin.

He felt the curve of her lips against his chest as she brushed against his cock from side to side.

Thank God she seemed to be as on board with sex as he was.

The water was done, and he reluctantly moved away to turn it off and to switch the jets on. He'd bought condoms on his way home the night before, hoping he'd get the chance to use them. He glanced toward the medicine cabinet where he'd stored the ones not in his nightstand or wallet.

She stepped into the water and groaned. "Oh my God. If I had one of these in my apartment, I'd never leave it."

He was absolutely fine with her spending as much time as she pleased in his big bathtub.

"I only use this tub when I get my ass kicked. But with you around, I can see other, better uses."

He joined her, settling her in between his thighs. Funny, he had this moment as they sat together, the steam from the water rising between them, he'd never realized how unsettled he'd been until she had walked into his building and everything had sort of clicked into place. Not even a full two days ago. Christ, how much in your life can change in such a short time.

For the first time in a long time, and certainly since she'd answered that call three days before, she felt...all right. Being there with him soothed her. Made her feel safe.

Which was silly. Of course she was capable of taking care of herself. But it was novel, being taken care of for a change.

It was probably stupid to like it. Certainly to get used to it. They all seemed to talk like she'd simply move up to Portland. Which she supposed meant he wanted more than a fun weekend with her.

She didn't know what she wanted. She had a life in Roseburg. A job she liked but was growing increasingly unhappy with because of the attitudes of her boss. Being here made her realize maybe it wasn't enough.

"Want to share whatever's got you thinking so hard your muscles are bunching up? I know you're worried about Allie." He spoke softly, his hands sliding up her arms where he began to knead her shoulders.

"You're really good with your hands," she nearly purred, relaxing into him.

He laughed. That laugh men do when they're really thinking about sex. It sent a thrill through her. It wasn't that she didn't think the next stop was bed. She was lying in his tub naked, between his thighs, his cock hard at the small of her back.

But he owned his sexuality in a way that rendered her a little breathless with anticipation. And that laugh, mmm.

"Restless I guess." Which was the truth on several levels.

"Why do I get the feeling you mean more than just about Allie? Talk to me."

"I'm not ready to yet. I'm mulling it all over."

"When you're like this, I realize how much I missed you all these years."

That made her laugh. "How so? Naked? Between your legs?"

He laughed too, brushing a kiss at her temple. "I have not been like this with anyone. Not since you. Did you...never mind."

"Did I sit in the bathtub and talk about my feelings with Mark?"

"I don't have a right to know. It's okay."

"He was a good man. *Is* a good man. He loved me, and in my own way I guess I loved him too." She paused, wondering about taking the risk of stripping herself bare. "But I couldn't share a big part of my life with him. Or, well I could have, but I didn't trust him with it. And I didn't trust you with it either, back then. But I can be who I am when I'm with you, and that is something I've never had with anyone but Allie, and not...well not like this."

The fingers that had been kneading stopped as he encircled her shoulders and pulled her close. "I'm surrounded by wolves every day. But until I looked into your eyes yesterday, I didn't realize how lonely I was. I have missed you so much. Because I have always talked to you and you've always listened. But the adult Michelle? You're beyond alluring. I know you have a case.

And I know you have a life, but when this is settled, I want you to consider there's something up here for you. I'm part of it."

She wanted to accept. Wanted to spin and say yes and fall into his arms and be his. But sudden didn't begin to describe what the situation was.

"This is moving so fast."

"I've known you since you were twelve and I was fourteen. You were my first. My first everything. This isn't fast. This is slow. Long and simmering. Until we were both in a different place. Enough to appreciate it maybe. I left in a dickish way and—"

She interrupted. "I understand. I hated you for it then. I thought it was about me. That I wasn't worth it. Before I knew the why, I mean. But even at that, when I saw you yesterday none of it mattered anymore."

He squeezed her a little tighter. "I'm sorry again that I gave you cause to think it was about you. It was about me but it was stupid how I did it. Your saying all this means a lot. Now that you're here...if you walked out of my life I'd hate it."

They were silent for some time. She was sleepy and warm, and it felt right there in his arms.

"I'd hate it too. I don't understand it. The way you make me feel, I mean. I'm *not* a quick decision kind of person. It took me nearly a year to decide on what couch to buy."

He snorted. "Witches are control freaks."

"We are? Or I am?"

"Every witch I've ever met. I should have remembered back to what you were like in high school. Is your room still brutally organized?"

"If you put everything where it's supposed to go, you can always find it later."

"I love how prim you are when you say that. Water's getting cold. Should I top us off with more hot or are you ready to get out?"

"I don't know. What are your plans if we get out?"

He slid his hands under the water to take her breasts in his hands, flicking his thumbs over her nipples. "Depends on what you'll let me do to you?"

"I'm pretty sure you've got a blank check in that department."

"Hm. I have credit? Nice."

He spun her, and she went to her knees as he caged her with those powerful thighs.

"You're crazy-hot when you're clothed, but naked? I'm not sure I'll survive." His grin was nearly a leer, and it filled her with a rush of emotion. Joy, lust, amusement, affection. She tipped her head back and laughed.

She wanted him. Even if it was only for a brief period of time before they both went back to their lives.

He stood, and she wrapped her legs around him to keep from falling. Not that she didn't enjoy all that strength. Good gracious.

"A girl could get used to a man in her bed with werewolf strength," she murmured as he wrapped a towel around them both and carried her through an adjacent doorway and into his bedroom.

He laid her on the bed and took her in from head to toe with so much raw desire on his features her breath got caught.

"So fucking beautiful."

She blushed but soaked up all the attention in any case. His cock, wow, she really couldn't seem to stop returning her attention to it. Rock hard and ready.

She licked her lips, and he groaned, tearing her attention from his cock to his face.

"I want to take my time with you and you go staring and it makes me forget the slow."

"You gonna use that on me?" She nodded at his cock, and his grin made things south of her belly button tighten and get wetter.

"You wanted me to help you forget. It's probably going to take a few hours."

She caught her bottom lip between her teeth as he bent and took her left foot in his hands. His big, strong hands.

"Either you have a thing for having your feet touched or I did something else you really like. Your pussy smells so good, Michelle."

"Hands," she gasped out as he nuzzled her instep and his stubble scratched that sensitive skin in all the right ways. "I have a thing." She moaned as he kissed her ankle and bent her leg, his lips moving along her calf.

"A thing about hands?"

He got to his knees on the bed and kept kissing her calf, pausing at her knee before switching to the other foot and leg.

"Yes." A breathy gasp that meant more than just his question. Yes to whatever he wanted. However he wanted it.

She'd never wanted anyone the way she did right then. Not even back in the day when she had him. Things were different. They were different, and yet, he knew her in a way no one else on the planet did and it was enough.

He gripped her tighter, sliding the aforementioned hands up her legs to her thighs, spreading them wide and holding her that way.

She nearly choked at the way it felt.

"I'm not sure I truly appreciated the heightened sense of scent I have until right this moment when your pussy got even hotter and wetter when I did that."

She had to close her eyes a moment. She'd never actually had a man use dirty talk during sex. It was totally underrated.

He settled against her, lying on top of her but keeping most of his weight off. It was...good to be held down like that.

His mouth met hers with similar strength, his teeth nipped her lip before his tongue swept inside like it was meant to be there.

His muscles bunched and relaxed as he moved against her, stroking against her skin. Her magick rose, unbidden, bringing a gasp as she knew it drifted over his body like a caress.

He opened his eyes slowly, carefully, the normal color having bled into that otherworldly green of his wolf.

"Your magick is nearly as tasty as your skin." The burr of his wolf was there. Her magick liked it. She realized her magick seemed to be apart from her as well as an integral part of her existence. It wanted *his* magick.

"I've never been with a witch before." He tipped his head back and breathed in deep. "I like it. Whatever you're doing with your magick, I mean. The rest of you is something I like too."

She tried to laugh but got lungs full of his scent, and she writhed beneath him, bringing the sharpness of his gaze back to her.

Was it him? The combo of him and her? Was it her magick and his? Whatever it was, like him, she'd never experienced it before. Maybe it was because she'd never had sex with another Other, and it was always like this. But given his response she didn't think it was that either.

"I'm not doing it on purpose. It would seem my magick really likes your wolf. Or something like that. Don't let this go to your head, but it's never been like this with anyone else."

His smile though, wow. Her nipples ached when he gave her that look.

"How can that not go to my head?" He shimmied down her body a little, licking over her nipples until heat rolled through her, leaving her nearly boneless.

She supposed he had a point. But she couldn't think about it right then with the edge of his teeth against her nipple.

"You're really good at that." She didn't even recognize her own voice as wave after wave of pleasure rolled through her. It had to be the stress and grief of the last days. Or something. Or maybe two Others getting down? Whatever.

"You're overthinking. I can tell." He kissed the swell beneath her nipple and then licked and kissed down her ribs and the hollow at her hipbone.

She laughed, but it strangled into a moan as he breathed warm air over her pussy but didn't stop, continuing to kiss his way over to the other hip.

"I'm not! I can't even speak much less think in any coherent way."

Her fingers slid into his hair, and she held on and tried not to order him to get those kisses and licks to the right.

"I only want you to think about this." He took a long, slow lick through her pussy and up to her clit that stole her breath.

"No problem," she managed to say, though her words were barely intelligible.

He slid his tongue up into her, making her arch on a gasp.

His fingers dug into the flesh of her ass, holding her up as if to serve himself of her body. All while he continued to devastate her pussy with his mouth.

It wasn't like she was small or delicate. At just a hair under five and a half feet tall she had been shorter than most of her boyfriends. But Josh was just so *big*. His strength, the ease with which he held her and did what he wanted with her body made her shiver with delight.

He shifted a little, finding her clit with that tongue of his. Swirl and suck, swirl and suck until she couldn't stop the *"please"* from escaping her lips as she tugged him closer by the hair still in her hands.

Orgasm shot through her as she gasped, nearly drowning in it as it sucked her down over and over until he laid her down gently with a kiss to her thigh before settling in next to her, pulling her close.

"I don't think I was very good at this the last time we were together. But I think I may have earned another chance."

She couldn't help it, she laughed. "Considering that most boys didn't eat pussy at all? I don't recall thinking you sucked at it. But certainly if you had, the job you just did would have erased all red marks on your record. Once my teeth stop tingling, we can get back to it. Hopefully by then I'll have regained muscle control."

She had no idea what it meant to hear so much satisfied pleasure in her tone. His woman, satisfied. The shadow of her earlier distress had been pushed away for a time. He'd made it better. She'd allowed him to.

Her taste lived in him. On his skin, on lips and tongue. Her climax had sent a rush of magick and scent through his system, and he wanted to roll around in it. Christ, it was heady stuff. He hadn't been drunk in a very long time. Wolves weren't really able to get drunk given the speed of their metabolisms, though a huge amount of alcohol or drugs could work for a brief period. That was usually something saved for emergencies though.

"Hearing you say pussy makes me really hard." He moved his weight, getting close enough to kiss her shoulder and then her mouth, which she'd turned to him.

She wrapped her arms around him, snuggling in, her body pressed to his as he kissed her lazily, taking his fill of her.

Ha. He wanted to gorge. To claim her until she was boneless and totally his. But that wasn't to be. Not for the time being. So he'd take his fill within limits.

She broke from his mouth and kissed down his throat, her teeth grazing the tendons where shoulder met neck and sending a shiver through his system. His wolf clutched her tighter, urging her to bite harder.

She licked over the tender skin, humming her satisfaction.

"I promise not to leave a mark," she murmured, moving to the hollow of his throat.

"Feel free to mark me all you like." His wolf would love it even more than he would.

"You're so hot I just want to take a bite."

He flipped her to her back, looming over her. She grinned up at him.

"It makes me hot when you bite me." He nipped her shoulder for emphasis. "It's..." he paused to taste the words he'd never said before, "...a flattering, sexy thing for a Were to be marked by his partner. Love bites, bite marks, whatever. And that it's you, makes it even better. So if you want to take a bite, go ahead on because I've got no complaints."

"Oh." Her grin slid into a nearly shy smile, and it tightened things low in his belly. She caught her bottom lip between her teeth for a moment. "I'd like to get back to work. I want to taste a lot more of you."

She did some fancy cop moves, and he was on his back again as she scrambled to all fours over his body.

She laid a trail of kisses over his chest, nipping here and there.

"Harder," he whispered.

Her pupils swallowed more color in her eyes. She liked that. The scent of her desire rose, underlining the point.

She bit him again on his biceps and he pushed into her teeth. She gave him more pressure until his hips jutted forward without him thinking about it.

Her gaze locked with his as she licked over the place she'd just bitten.

"*Goddamn,*" he snarled. "Don't want to wait. Want to be in you."

"Did you use to be this impatient?" She ignored his orders and kissed her way to the other nipple and then scooted down his body to his cock. Her gaze locked on his, she angled him and swirled her tongue around the head.

He strangled a reply and cleared his throat to repeat himself. "Was I, a teenage boy, impatient about sex?" He laughed. "I'm just grateful I wasn't so bad at it that you laughed in my face tonight."

She did something with her fingers just behind his balls, and his laugh died on what was probably a beg. And he was okay with that.

He couldn't tear his eyes away from the sight of her mouth taking the length of his cock in and pulling back, leaving it dark and slick.

He let it go on nearly too long, nearly too close to losing it and blowing down that pretty throat. But he hadn't lied, he wanted to fuck her so with a gasp and a draw on all his control, he took her shoulders and pushed her back.

"So good. Too good." He rolled over and grabbed a condom. He hadn't used one since college, but it wasn't like it was complicated. A quick tear of the top and it was on.

She had a smile on her mouth and he had to kiss it a bit. Which was good as he was able to wrest his need back a little.

The last thing he wanted was to come five seconds after he got inside her.

In fact...

"You on top, gorgeous. Or I'll find it a lot harder to go slow."

She straddled his waist, her hair a tumble around her face and shoulders, her skin dusted with her magick like glitter.

But when she slid down his cock with her cunt, squeezing, so hot that he had to bite back a curse, he had to suck in a breath before clenching his jaw. So good it dug into his gut, sending a burst of pleasure so intense through him that he broke out in a sweat.

Michelle's groan made it even better. And that was before she gripped his sides, her nails digging in as she began to move. Not up and down, but back and forth, rubbing herself against him as she kept him deep.

He wasn't the only one who'd learned a few things since those earlier, less-finessed days when they'd been together before. On one hand, he was clearly the beneficiary of that. She'd grown into a confident woman, and they had plenty of good times in bed ahead of them. That was a positive.

On the other, it meant she'd been with people who'd taught her this. Wolves were incredibly possessive of their mates. The thought of another man's hands on her made him want to yank the condom off and fill her full of *his* seed, marking her in as many ways as he could.

His wolf didn't care that the times had changed. That a modern man worth having wouldn't ever do such a thing. That part of his existence was all about urges and passion, deep, sweeping emotion, and it didn't care that humans didn't act that way.

And in the years since he'd been a wolf, the man had never had to struggle to control those urges the way he did right then, her pussy rippling around his cock as she rode him.

Her gaze had gone blurry and he arched to get her attention. She moaned and swallowed hard, her gaze sharpening and landing on his face.

"Hey there. You with me?"

She nodded, licking her lips.

"Good. You feel so amazing."

One corner of her mouth rose.

Her head tipped back, exposing the line of her body, gleaming with magick and sweat, the scent of all that mingling into a perfumed vise around him as he took her in. The points of her nipples on breasts that swayed slightly as she moved. The swell of her hips beneath his hands. The play of her muscles there, against his palms. He caught peeks of his cock as she undulated.

It was impossible that he could feel so much at once without simply exploding from it.

"More."

She moved to look into his face again.

"I'm here. You're inside me. Take what you need."

She had *no* idea what that statement did to him.

He rolled, staying buried in her pussy. She wrapped her legs around his waist and held on as he sped up his thrusts. Deeper. God. Harder.

She arched into him, her nails in his back, urging him on, rolling her hips to meet him each time he slid back into her cunt.

She made a noise in the back of her throat each time he got all the way in. He kissed her, hard, swallowing that sound.

"Make yourself come," he whispered into her mouth.

She sucked at his tongue and then let go of his shoulder with one hand.

Being with him felt so daring.

She'd never, ever made herself come in front of another person. Even when she was having sex with them.

He made her bold. Sexy. Like no matter what she said or wanted, he'd give to her without judging. Or even better, like it that way.

With him so deep inside, the moment she stroked her clit with her middle finger she was already halfway there. It was sooo good as he fucked into her body in such a raw way.

"Yes. God, you're hot." He brushed his mouth over her jaw and down her neck. "Tight. Wet. I'm close. Don't let me go first."

She sped her fingers, firmed her touch. His groan told her he felt the way she clamped down around his cock.

So full.

He angled, still thrusting, and sucked the skin on the side of her breast. Hard enough to make it nearly hurt. Hard enough and long enough to leave a mark.

That excited her more than she'd ever imagined such a thing could. And the edge she'd been walking dropped away and she plunged into climax with a snarl that matched his as he licked against her skin.

Thrusting several more times before he stopped, he remained buried deep with a long groan of her name.

He nuzzled the spot he'd given her a hickey for a moment. "I'll be right back."

Which is when she realized he'd used a condom. Dimly she remembered that Weres didn't transmit or catch STDs and that they had some sort of super smell that could tell when the female was fertile.

She shrugged to herself as she relaxed back into the bed. Maybe she'd dodged a bullet and her cycle was off. No matter.

The sex was just the thing she needed to burn off some of the anxiety that had drowned her for the last days.

He strolled back in looking delicious and wearing nothing but a smile. "Stay over?"

"I don't know. All my things are at the hotel."

"I have an extra toothbrush. I'll take you back first thing. You're tired and I'm tired and it's safe here. We can watch a movie if you like. Chill out. Everyone has your cell anyway. If something comes up, they'll call you."

She wanted to. More than she should have, and it sort of alarmed her how not alarmed she was.

It had been a long time since she'd slept with anyone. It appealed to her on several levels. She would be safe, yes. But not alone.

He climbed into bed and pulled her into his arms. "I can see the battle you're waging with yourself on your face. It's not weakness to want comfort. To let me help you. If it helps, it makes me feel better to comfort you. So there's that."

"You're irresistible, you know that?"

"Good. Because you are too. So? You'll stay? I have T-shirts you can wear. In the morning, I mean, because you should most definitely sleep naked. You don't need any panties though."

"Pushing it now," she said without any real heat.

He laughed and she snuggled closer, breathing him in.

Chapter Seven

She woke up with a start at the sound of hushed voices. It took a few moments, and a few breaths, to remember she was at Josh's place. The bedding smelled like him. Like them.

Smiling, she stretched and rolled from bed. He'd taken her twice more before she'd pretty much passed out, totally exhausted and relaxed.

But also a little sore. She needed a shower to help that, but for the moment she pulled herself together. She had her clothes from the day before, and he'd helpfully left a new toothbrush on the counter in his bathroom.

Before she got back into her bra, she looked at the love bites he'd left on the side of her breast. She brushed her fingers over them, a phantom tingle warming her even as her nipples hardened at the memory of the pull of his mouth, the scrape of his teeth. Who knew she'd find such a thing hot?

She washed her face and brushed her teeth before rooting through her purse to find a ponytail holder and enough makeup to do a passable job.

And okay, so she did peek a little. She had to find the brush after all, so she looked in a few drawers and his medicine cabinet. There were no girly anythings in the room. No hair gizmos. When she did locate his brush, it was one of those wooden man brushes. No tampons. Nothing to indicate a woman was a regular guest here.

She had no right, frankly no business even thinking about such a thing. But it pleased her nonetheless. Something had clicked between them and there wasn't any unringing that bell. She liked him. Liked the grown-up Josh.

A lot.

More than she should. She took forever to decide on what to order for dessert but there she stood in Josh's bathroom, and even though everything else in her life was upside down and speeding toward horror, she was sure of one thing and that was Josh.

She rolled her eyes at her reflection and went out to see who Josh was talking to.

A pert blonde stood in the living room with her hand on Josh's arm, and Michelle's jaw hurt from clenching it so hard. "Did I interrupt something?" She totally failed at sounding perky.

The woman's gaze slid to Josh, who'd turned, smiling at the sight of her.

He held out a hand, and she took it without thinking, letting him draw her closer. "I wanted to let you sleep as long as possible. Come meet Tracy Warden. She's one of my Alphas."

The stunning blonde turned a smile her way, moving away from Josh and holding her hand out to shake. "Josh has told us about you. It's nice to meet you."

So this Alpha had two mates. Probably no time to bone Josh. Which was stupid anyway, it's not like she owned him or anything.

Michelle shook Tracy's hand and smiled back. It was impossible not to really, Tracy Warden had the sort of manner you'd need to be a dick not to respond to in kind.

"I'm Michelle. I want to thank you for the help your pack has given me in this investigation. It would have taken me a lot longer, maybe it would have been impossible altogether for me to have gotten this far without it."

Which was totally true.

"Of course. We have to stick together. Especially now. These mages are a danger to us all. I was down the street at our offices, and I admit I wanted to stop by to check in and meet you in person. I spoke to my sister, she's the Enforcer for Cascadia, they've had some missing wolves. *We've* had I guess. I'm still Cascadia in my heart, even though I run my own pack now." She shrugged, concern on her face.

"I'm sorry to hear that."

"Owen has been a big help. They think there's something else at play. Something bigger."

A shiver roiled through her. "Worse than these mages working with turned witches?" That was hard to imagine, and truth be told, she sort of dreaded the thought of what could be worse than that.

"They're working on it. Whatever it is. But we've put out an order that all our wolves travel in twos or more. Safer to stick together."

If it scared things that turned into giant wolves who were fast and vicious, what the hell chance did witches stand?

Michelle blew out a breath. "I need to check in at work and then with Pam. She's been a big help, by the way. Josh, I know you have work to do with your pack, I'm fine on my own."

Tracy and Josh rolled their eyes in unison.

"Did you both just tag-team eye-roll me?"

Tracy looked to Josh and they both laughed. But a bit of tension threaded the sound. Something wasn't being said.

"Use my office." He pointed toward a door to the right of the living room. "I'm not going anywhere. I have a right hand. Damon is perfectly capable of holding down the fort when I'm out with you. If I'm ordering my wolves to travel in twos, do you really think I'd let you go out alone?"

He had a point. But.

"They don't even know I'm here."

"Of course they do." Josh cleared his throat. "Go, make your calls and check in. I'm going to do the same. Tracy and I need to talk about a few things. We'll talk when you have an idea of what you need to do today."

She gave him side eye, but let it go. For the time being.

"It was nice to meet you, Tracy."

Tracy smiled at her. "Me too. I'm sure we'll see each other again soon. I was just telling Josh we were having a pack dinner tomorrow night. We're a raucous bunch, but though I'm biased, we're all pretty fun. And, Gabe, he's one of my mates, he's an amazing cook so it's worth it."

"Oh. Um. Maybe. Thanks for the invite. I appreciate it."

"Gina will be there. The other Owen witches who live in the area tend to come to our events. Safety in numbers and they're hours away from Seattle. I know they're all excited to meet you. I hear you met Gina yesterday. She's awesome, isn't she?"

Michelle was nearing her *whoa too much* point. So much stuff flying at her at once. She knew her magick began to rise, which was odd because she rarely had this problem at home. Then again, at home she wasn't really around any Others aside from Allie and her mom. Even Michelle's mom wasn't much for working her Craft.

Josh reached out and took her hand, squeezing, and her panic ebbed some. "Go. I know it's a lot. We'll talk more later. I'll bring you some coffee in a bit."

She nodded and smiled at Tracy as she headed into Josh's office, closing the door behind herself. She leaned there for a few long moments, getting herself together.

Over ninety-six hours had passed. Four days since Kathy's call had turned Michelle's life inside out. Every minute now was a little bit of luck in finding Allie slipping away.

She chose the desk in the room that looked like it was used less and sat, grabbing a nearby pad and pen, and called Roseburg.

She spoke to her boss.

"Anything new?"

"No. Other than the canvass of the apartment complex." Which she knew about because Michelle had been the one who organized it after all.

Dexter continued on, shuffling papers at his desk as he spoke. "No further sightings. The plates are still on watch, but since the last sighting in Portland there's been nothing. She hasn't been seen. Her ATM card hasn't been used. What about you?"

She sighed. "Nothing else. We did a canvass in an area the SUV was last seen. Portland PD helped with some manpower." Dexter was a good cop, but he hated shifters. She hadn't divulged any of the help she'd received from Pacific. He'd been active in a campaign to change hiring practices in city government to ban shifters. On one hand she wanted to tell him all about how much assistance Others had been so she could say, *see, they're good people who help*. But reality told her he'd shut down and stop believing anything she said.

"We didn't find anything. I'm going in today to speak to the guy they took into custody at the scene of the murder in the convenience store the SUV was seen at."

"Bunch of paranormal violence, that. Probably a shifter. I saw the pictures. Nothing human coulda done that. You just keep out of their business. You think Allie was tied up in it? Could be why she up and got herself taken. Hell, maybe she left with them."

Her magick rose hard and fast. So hard her esophagus burned and several things rattled in the office around her.

"What did you just say to me?"

Josh burst in, his magick mixing with hers. His wolf shone through his eyes.

She held her hand up to keep him quiet. "Did you just blame the victim of a kidnapping? My best friend?"

"Alls I'm saying is, you get what you get when you go mixing with them what's causing all this ruckus."

"With all due respect, *sir*, Allie was taken against her will. All the evidence we have points to that. Whether or not she was involved with anyone or anything paranormal has absolutely nothing to do with our duty to find her."

"Sure. You need to come back. You said yourself you haven't found anything. Let Portland PD keep an eye out. Question the guy and come back to work. There are cases we need you on here. Whether you want to admit it or not, our missing person is just one of many."

She hung up. Without saying goodbye. She shook so hard, her nails dug into her palms until the scent of blood hit, and Josh was on his knees in front of her, taking her hands.

"What's going on? Talk to me, Michelle, because I'm about to lose my shit. You already have. What is happening?"

She thought about what to say. Her boss's prejudices bothered her. Embarrassed her even. It was hard enough on her being a witch, but Josh was a shifter and she didn't want to hurt him. At the same time, she needed to talk.

"No new clues on Allie. My boss wants me back in Roseburg. I don't think he cares about Allie at all. He's...he's a bigot, and since he's seen the pictures from the murder at the convenience store, he's convinced shifters are involved and he's pretty much written Allie off as a 'shifter lover' who gets what she deserves for mixing with Weres."

He growled. "Are you going back?"

"Not without finding her."

"Don't go at all." He kissed her fists until she relaxed and unclenched. He hissed when he saw the half-moon wounds. He kissed them too. "I know it's not just me. You feel it too. This connection between us."

"I don't know what I feel."

He locked his gaze with hers. "Liar. You're too brave to be such a liar, Michelle."

"Okay, to be honest, I don't know all the words for all I feel. Yes, there is a connection. But I have a life in Roseburg. I can't just walk away."

"Why not? Since I've been gone have you and your mom gotten close?"

She snorted. "No."

"Your boss is a bigot. What happens when he finds out you're a witch? You and I both know the coming out of witches and Vampires is only a matter of time. You can't hide it. Not anymore. I'm shocked it hasn't happened before now."

She blew out a breath. In truth, though she loved being a cop, she didn't love her workplace because of Dexter. Sure he liked her now, but once he found out...well Josh was right. And it was toxic to deal with his ranty views all the time.

"He'll leave one day. My boss I mean. The next person could be better."

He shook his head. "I want you here. With me. There's a police department here and several in the surrounding suburbs. You're smart and Pam has friends all over the place. Be with me."

"This is so sudden. I don't know!"

"You're a witch." He laughed, kissing her wrists. "You can move stuff with power you draw from the earth. How is this thing, which isn't sudden by the way, I've known you longer than anyone else I'm not related to, less real because you feel it after reconnecting with me a few days ago? We are beings of magick."

He kissed her forehead. "I know things. I accept things. Some things just *are*, and the way I feel about you is what it is. I know you, Michelle. I can see your passion and your strength. Your determination to find your friend. I admire you a great deal. You've always been beautiful. But Michelle as a woman is a far more alluring creature. Give us a chance. You have nothing in Roseburg. A shitty boss. A job that you can do here. Be here. With me."

He was right. She just knew things sometimes. Despite her cautious nature when it came to making big leaps of faith, this connection she had with Josh was real. Immense. And it could be something amazing and forever.

"We both grew up in the human world. I understand that you're hesitant. But my wolf is my magick. I can feel the threads to you, between us. My wolf knew it immediately. I loved you back then, of course. But I was a kid. I had a lot of growing up to do. I'm a better person now. The thought of you going back to Roseburg drives me nuts. I understand it's your home. But...I'm asking you to try to make one here. With me. For us. There are Others here. Witches who you can bond with and get to know. Understand your gifts in a whole new way. My pack, which is my family, they'd accept you, open their door to you. You deserve that. Not some asshole who would throw away a young woman who'd been kidnapped because she might be or have been involved with Others."

She licked her lips. The allure of everything he offered was overwhelming. She'd been lonely a long time. Yes, she had Allie, but that was pretty much it. If she pretended to be human, she could have more. But she wasn't. And the older she got, the more she understood that. And the more that understanding left her empty, aching for something else. Connection. Community.

She'd known him since she'd been a child. He'd been part of her life pretty much every day, and then he'd been gone and for over a decade that had defined part of her too. But maybe his absence had steeled her for what they could have if she accepted what she knew as true even though common sense said this was too fast.

"I'll think about it. I'm not going back to Roseburg before I find her. I have vacation time. A lot of it. I'll call in and use that. I need to focus on Allie right now. Do you understand?"

He nodded. "I'll do everything I can, offer all the assistance in my power to help."

"Is Tracy still here?"

He shook his head and stood, pulling her up with him. "She left a few minutes ago. Let's go get this cleaned up." He indicated the nail gouges on her palms.

"I need to call Pam first. I want to speak to Charlie."

Josh sighed. "I'd tell you that you already spoke to him and that he's not going to tell you anything else. But I can see that would be a waste of time."

"I'm glad we're on the same page."

"First let me deal with your palms. Okay?"

She followed him into his bathroom, and he pulled out a first aid kit while she washed her hands. "It's not that big a deal. Just some scratches. It's not life threatening."

He made a growl, picking her up and putting her on the counter, stepping between her thighs. She allowed him to dry her hands gently and pour antiseptic on them, patting them dry once more.

"Why do you have a first aid kit anyway? I mean you guys heal pretty fast."

He grinned. "Pretty fast isn't instant. My job is bloody. Not always, but frequent enough that it's good to have supplies on hand."

"Are you seeing anyone?" She blurted this out and felt the heat on her face.

"No. Well." He gave her that smile that did things to all her pink parts. "I am, but that's you. So you don't have to be jealous of yourself." He kept working until he'd lightly bandaged her wounds and let go, leaning close to kiss her.

He'd actually only meant to kiss her quickly but she responded, that delicious rush of her magick enveloping him. Wrapping around his cock like a fist. He stepped closer, she wrapped her legs around him, holding him there as he took her mouth. Drowned in her taste. Wallowed in it until his cock throbbed in time with his thundering pulse.

He broke away, sucking in air as he pulled her hair from the ponytail, running his fingers through it. He hadn't intended to ask her to stay. He'd been trying very hard to take it slow, at a human pace. But her jealous reaction when she'd come out and seen Tracy's hand on his arm had roused his wolf. His wolf didn't give one fuck about waiting. He wanted Michelle.

And her upset at her boss's behavior and talk of going back to Roseburg had been more than he could process without saying at least something.

He knew she'd heard him. Agreed even. Knew too, that she was processing and felt it too fast. But fuck fast. He knew what he knew and this woman was his. Had been his all along.

He pulled her shirt up and off, tossing it to the floor, her bra following. She arched with a gasp into his hands as he found her nipples, tugging them between thumb and forefinger. He groaned when he caught sight of his marks on them.

Driven to claim, to pleasure and taste, one handed, he pulled her pants open and down.

Her heartbeat sped, her pupils enlarged, her skin flushed—she was with him all the way. Thank God.

"Your smell," he growled as he slid his fingers through her pussy, wet and hot. Ready for him. "Makes me want to shove my face into your cunt and lap you up for hours. I want it on my face and my hands, wrapped around my cock. You're delicious."

Her breath came out in a stutter, and that scent bloomed as the hot scald of that honey coated his fingertips.

"Fuck me," she whispered.

"Oh, I will. First you need to come. Then I'll fuck you. Your pleasure is my job. Lean back against the mirror behind you."

She did as he turned his hand, sliding two fingers into her and rubbing the pad of his thumb against her clit over and over.

"Don't undo all my work on your hands, beautiful. You can scratch me up later."

She started to laugh, but it ended on a snarled plea as he pressed a little harder on her clit.

"You want to come? Hm?"

"Yes!"

He leaned in, licking and biting her nipples as he sped the fingers thrusting into her cunt, his thumb pressing over her clit in time with the suck and pull until she exploded in a rush of honey and magick.

He wanted her so much he barely even remembered the condom as she unbuttoned and unzipped his pants, pulling his cock out.

"Hands back or I'm gonna lose it."

He rolled the condom on and was fully seated in a breath, then moved to utter stillness as she clutched and fluttered all around his cock.

He did note a bit of discomfort on her face when he first started fucking her. "Sore?"

"A little. It's been..." She laughed. "I'm not used to that much fucking in one night."

"Should I stop? I don't want to—"

His sentence died as she used the legs wrapped around him to haul him back in deep. "No. I'll have to maim you if you stop. The hurt is gone. Now it's all..." She hummed and it slid over his skin. "It's all pleasure now. I promise."

Chapter Eight

She took a long, hot shower after their impromptu sex on his bathroom counter. She should have been embarrassed, but really, what was the point in denying it? She wanted him. Like, a lot. When they'd been together before, they'd had this same sort of intense physical connection, but they hadn't had the opportunity to rut like rabbits. No place to be alone that often.

Clearly they still had it, which made her a little more at ease with their earlier discussion. Her attraction to him wasn't sudden. It had always been there. Only now they had doors to lock and get naked behind.

He knocked on the bathroom door and came in as she was turning the water off.

"Two things. Damon just brought over all your stuff from the hotel. I'll leave the bag in here so you can change into clean stuff. I have a washer and dryer if you have things you need to wash. And two, Pam called and said you could come by in an hour to interview the prisoner."

"He brought all my stuff?" She got out and took the towel he handed her way.

"And checked you out. You'll stay here. It's safest and I like it."

She arched a brow. "He checked me out of my hotel room. Without asking me?"

Josh's features changed and he put his hands up. "It's safest here. Surely you can't argue with that."

"Well I certainly can't if no one even bothers to ask me about it."

She wrapped the towel around her body and riffled through her bag until she found clean underwear and pulled them on, finding her bra, which he'd picked up from the floor and folded on the counter. He watched as she got dressed.

"I'm sorry I didn't ask. There's something you should know. While I'm not an alpha at Tracy, Nick and Gabe's level, I am an alpha wolf in general. My job, the place I hold in the pack, is one of protection. It's hardwired into me. I do things to protect the people I care about. You're one of those people. I act and forget about the permission part."

That was a bald truth. She looked him up and down, and her body came to life again. She knew *he* knew because his nostrils flared and he got that face. Oh he was going to be such a handful if she went forward with any sort of relationship with him.

Which seemed a given. Because she liked him. And maybe the protective, bossy thing he had. Though it would not do to give him even an inch. A man like him would run right over a woman in the name of protecting her if she didn't push him back when he stepped over the line.

"Here's the deal, Joshua. No one makes my decisions but me. As it happens, I agree it's probably safer here than in a hotel. Given our...relationship status, it seems stupid for me to go to the expense of a hotel when I sleep here anyway. But that does not mean you can make my choices. I am not down with that, no matter how good you are at making me come. You got me?"

He moved to her, pulling the towel from her hands and drying her hair. He bent to kiss her shoulder. "I got you. Thank you."

"How long will it take to get to the jail where I'll be interviewing Charlie? I'll have to check in and turn over my weapon and all that stuff so add time to the travel for that."

"We should leave in about twenty minutes. Can you be ready?"

"Yes. But you can't be in here or I'll get distracted."

"I'll shower while you get ready." He peeled his clothes off, and she made herself stop looking and get dressed.

On the drive over, she watched the city out the window as she thought. She realized he'd yet again used a condom. She knew her body pretty well, and she was pretty sure she wasn't fertile. How did you broach *that* in a conversation though? He'd begged her to stay in Portland to be with him so it wasn't that he was grossed out by her.

A shiver went through her as she remembered what he'd said about her scent.

He made a sound next to her as he drove, and she looked over. One corner of his mouth was turned up as supremely male satisfaction was stamped on his features.

"I love that I can scent when you're turned on. You're an incredibly sexual woman. I like that."

He kept his eyes on the road, and she was glad because she blushed down to her toes.

"What if I was thinking about Daniel Craig or something? You're pretty ballsy to assume you're who I was thinking about." She hmpfed and he laughed, reaching out to tangle his fingers with hers.

"Ah, but you aren't thinking of Daniel Craig. You're thinking about me. Just like I'm thinking about you. Remembering the way you felt around me this morning as I fucked you."

"If I stay in Portland, how am I ever going to get any work done if you get me hot and bothered all the time?" she mumbled.

"It's my pleasure to get you hot and bothered. But I assume you'd get a job and I won't be with you every moment so hopefully there'll be no horny pussy when I'm not there. I don't share."

There was a pause just then. Not a spoken one. But she felt it in his demeanor.

"What?"

"Huh?" He turned down a street. "The jail is this way. Pam said to call her when we parked so can you do that now? She'll be waiting so she can escort us through."

She let it go and grabbed her phone, making the call. Pam, true to her word, met them, escorting Michelle through.

"Josh, you need to wait here," Pam said quietly.

He grimaced and his wolf showed. "No, I can't. I need to be with Michelle."

"You're not a cop. We're in cop central, it's not like anything is going to happen to me." Michelle probably should have been annoyed by his bossiness, but she must have been crazy because it worked for him and she was flattered and touched more than annoyed.

Pam nodded. "Wait here. We'll be out when we finish. Or go to Pacific and do your work, and I'll bring her over when I finish."

"I'm not going anywhere." He turned to Michelle. "You will be careful."

"I'll do my best. Me being all helpless and stuff."

Pam fought a smile but managed to hold it back.

Josh snorted. "I know you're more than capable of taking care of yourself. I'll see you in a bit."

It was hard to remain flustered when he was so adorable so she let it go, telling herself she'd have to continue to get used to how protective he was.

They followed him to a group of chairs in the lobby, preparing to leave him there until they'd finished with Charlie. Michelle pulled her cop all around herself like armor and turned to Pam. "I'm ready."

But all hell broke loose before they could get on the elevators.

Cops rushed past and she felt it. Dark, ugly magic was being worked.

Michelle turned to Pam. "Shit. Get me to where he is. Now."

"There's a lockdown. I can't override it."

"They're here. The mages. Something ugly is being worked." She gagged, and Josh was at her side, touching her.

"What is happening?"

"Get Charlie safe. They're here for him."

Josh took her upper arms in his hands and shook, once, to get her attention. "What if they're here for you? Have you thought of that?"

A blast of something very dark sent her to her knees. She heard shouts about a prisoner being down, and she knew. Josh pulled her out of the way of the traffic, shielding her with his body. Pam had rushed off to get information.

"What? Should I call Gina? Damn it, Michelle are you all right? Answer me!"

"Charlie is dead. Or close to it. I...my skills aren't that good, but I can tell that much."

He patted her all over. "Are you all right? Did it hurt you?"

She pushed his hands back. She was a cop on the floor for God's sake. "I need to stand up, and you need to back off or get kicked in the sac."

He relaxed a little, standing and letting her do so without his assistance. "If you're threatening to kick me in the junk, you must be all right."

Pam hustled over. "Another prisoner killed Charlie. They were walking him to an interview room. He was in cuffs and with two guards and another prisoner walked up and snapped his neck. The other prisoner is dead too. He'd been shot several times because he wouldn't stop. They didn't injure anyone else. I...this is beyond my skill level."

Hers too.

He led her to his office at Pacific. She was still pale, and his wolf noted the remnants of whatever spell that'd knocked her to the ground. Her scent was slightly off. A little dirty. And not the good kind of dirty.

"Michelle, I'd like you to meet someone."

She looked up from where she'd been studying her phone. "Sorry. I was texting with Gage. They're going to get in contact with Gina, and she's going to call me when they get all that figured out."

"No need to be sorry." Gabe stepped into the office and the room seemed to shrink around them. "I'm Gabe Murphy. Tracy said she met you earlier. I wanted to stop in and introduce myself and extend our offer of help. Are you well?"

He took Michelle's hand, and before Josh knew what he was doing, he'd put himself in Gabe's path, showing his teeth.

His back was to her so she wouldn't have seen anything, but Gabe sure did. But rather than be upset or offended, he had to wrestle back a grin. Josh narrowed his eyes, promising retribution, friend to friend, if he got any teasing about this.

Josh made himself step to the side, placing his hand on Michelle's shoulder. Her brows were up as she glanced back and forth between them both.

"Sorry, wolf stuff." Gabe shrugged, his smile still in place.

She took his hand, shaking it.

"If you don't mind my saying so, you don't look well." Gabe examined her closely.

"The spell that was used was...wrong. Gage told me it should wear off in a bit."

"How about you eat something? I was just about to head home to see my babies. Why don't you and Josh come along? Nick said he was going to grab some Chinese on the way to meet us. I'll call and tell him to get extra."

"Gabe, Nick and Tracy have two daughters. And a dopey three-legged dog named Milton who guards them with his life."

Gabe laughed. "He's really fond of all the food they drop. What do you say? You can fill us in on what you know. Maybe we can brainstorm something."

"Are you sure?"

Gabe smiled, charming. "Of course. Nick would only whine about me and Tracy having met you and him not yet. He's a handful that way."

Her phone rang. "Excuse me a moment. This is Gina."

She answered and turned to where she'd been sitting at his desk.

"Are you all right?" Gina asked.

Michelle took a deep breath. "I think so."

"I'd like to see you. To do a quick check of your shields and your aura. I want to be sure you're unharmed. I know Gage told you we're learning all this as we go."

"Tell her to come to my house for lunch. She can check you there." Gabe announced this without so much as a *pardon me* for listening in on your phone call.

"You'll get used to that. Tell him what your limits are. He might even remember it. But don't count on it. Wolves, especially male wolves, are ridiculously overprotective. I'll grab Damon and we'll meet you at their place in a few."

She hung up and looked back at both men, who stood, arms crossed over their chests, only making them appear more imposing.

"I've seen that one before. Lots of perps do that." She put the phone into her pocket and stood. She was still a little dizzy but at least nausea had retreated some and she didn't have double vision anymore. "Also, it's rude to eavesdrop."

Josh grinned at Gabe, who raised a brow.

"Gina is right. We're really nosy and overprotective. We have great hearing so it's hard *not* to eavesdrop on a phone call. It comes in handy sometimes though. There's a bright side."

Gabe Murphy appeared to be a bigger handful than Josh, which said a lot. Little tiny Tracy must be a powerhouse to keep him in line.

"We'll meet you at your place." Josh nodded at Gabe, who waved one last time and disappeared.

"If you need to rest, they have extra bedrooms. It's a soothing place they've got. Warded by the Owen witches just months back. It's safe and quiet. It'll do you good. You'll like Nick."

"They're your family, right? So this is like…meeting your dad? Your other dad, since I already met Gabe."

He took her face in his hands and kissed her quickly. "Sort of, I guess. Don't be nervous, all right?"

She sighed as he took her bag. "Maybe if this last week hadn't been filled with kidnapping, dark magic, attacks and death, I might be more worried. At this point, I'm just happy to be somewhere no one will try to kill me for a little while." She looked him askance. "No one will, right? I mean there's no battle to the death or anything like that?"

He burst out laughing as they headed out to his car. "Nope. Just a dog, some toddlers and alpha wolves."

One of the girls, Rose, the two-year-old, had settled next to Michelle, reaching out to pat her hand from time to time. It was pretty freaking adorable. And it eased some of her nervousness.

Not that anyone had given her anything to be nervous about. Tracy, Nick—who looked like a model—and Gabe had been incredibly welcoming. Josh had stuck close. The girls were sweet and jolly, and the house was, just as Josh had said, soothing and calm, even with all the people in it.

People. Ha. Weres had so much energy. Power coming off them in waves. She'd have known the difference in a crowd, between a human and a shifter. Funny how she never noticed it before. There had to be shifters in Roseburg for goodness' sake, she'd just never been in any enclosed space or near enough to one. Or maybe she didn't notice, or attribute it to any one person in particular.

Whatever the case, when Gina arrived with another Owen witch, Rhonda, it was easy enough to tell the difference between their energy signatures.

Rhonda was a nurse much like Allie, and it sent a slice of sadness through Michelle at the thought.

"Let's take a look at you." Gina looked back over her shoulder to Tracy. "Can we use the office down here? It's hard to get a good read with all this magick around."

"Oh, of course!" She opened the door and let them in. Rhonda closed it and magick rushed through the room.

"I'm just going to look you over, all right?"

Michelle nodded, watching Rhonda and Gina, seeing how they drew energy and used it.

It didn't take very long, less than three minutes or so, before Rhonda's gaze sharpened and she looked into Michelle's eyes.

"You're all right. Nothing permanent. I expect you'll feel nauseated for a bit. Whatever was done was unnatural. A gross misuse of energy and power. It'll rebound eventually if the caster was human or witch. I don't know though. There's something else here that seems more than stolen magic. This is..." Rhonda licked her lips as she thought. "To aim a spell like that, to cause one person to harm another, much like what they did in the convenience store, it takes a lot of power and focus to do something like that."

"Do you think there's something else helping? Another sort of paranormal we don't know about?"

"We need to talk to Gage and Lark about this. And Josh too. He'll want to protect the pack, as will the Alphas." Gina ran hands through her hair and still looked gorgeous afterward. If Michelle had done that she'd look like a hobo.

"Let's have Josh come in when we call Gage. I don't want the children to hear."

"Good idea."

She went out to get Josh, Gina right behind her, but found yet *another* woman touching him when they got to the dining room. Only this one wasn't touching him like a friend. She looked up into his face like she wanted him to kiss her, and her back was arched like she was trying to brush her boobs against him.

Something hot and unpleasant ran through her veins at the sight.

Tracy was speaking quietly to Josh and the woman, but it was Josh who turned and started. "Michelle."

"So glad you remembered my name. I'm going to make a call to Owen. I thought someone from the pack might want to be present. If you're not too busy." She turned and walked back into the office.

Gina closed the door and leaned against it. "I need to talk to you about this whole thing. Wolves are...casual about their affections. But with the one—the one as in the *forever* one—it's different."

Josh tried to open the door, Gina poked her head out. "Back off. I'll let you know when you can come in." And closed it in his face.

He knocked. "Michelle, let me in. I want to explain."

"Wolves. Pushiest motherfuckers on Earth." Gina opened again. "Do you need to be put on a time-out? Back. Off." This time Michelle heard Tracy's laugh as she told Josh to be patient.

"As I was saying. I know who the female with Josh just now is. She's been into Josh for years. But he's never made any promises to her. You are not her. Do you understand?"

Michelle shook her head. "No. I don't. It wasn't anything. I just felt...jealous, I guess. It sucks. I don't like it."

Gina laughed. "Gurl. I hear you. It's part of that connection you have with Josh. I can see it. Anyone can. I'm trying to say...God, how do I say this?"

Michelle rolled her eyes. "Josh got around. There will be lots of ladies everywhere we go who've taken him for a long ride."

Both of them laughed at that.

"Be that as it may. You are not them. The difference will be apparent immediately if he's standing with you. Word will get out. Once people know he's, um, in a relationship with you, a real one, they'll back off. Wolves are orderly even as they are bossy and possessive and overbearing. Our wolves anyway. There are beta wolves. Damon and Josh aren't that kind."

Gina took Michelle's hand and squeezed it. "I like you. We're glad you're around and we want to keep it that way. We understand that a lot of this will be new to you and we just want to help. Explain what we can, when it's necessary."

"So the blonde out there used to bang Josh, but now that I'm around she'll stop petting him?"

Rhonda laughed. "Yes, you'll fit in just fine."

Josh came into the office. "If you don't mind." He gave Gina a look and she waved it away. "I'd like to talk to Michelle alone for a few minutes."

Rhonda and Gina strolled out. "They heal pretty fast," Gina called out as she shut the door in her wake, leaving them alone.

"Did she just encourage you to kick me or something?"

"Depends. Did you do something you need kicking over?"

He took a deep breath and stepped closer. "No. Will you let me explain?"

She shrugged, feeling like a dumbass.

"I was not a virgin when you came to Portland. You ought to know, I lost it with you anyway. She's my past. On and off. Never serious."

"Did you use a condom with her too?" Holy shit. Did she actually say that out loud?

He stilled. "What?"

"I don't know an awful lot about shifters, but I do know they don't get or give STDs and they can scent when a female is fertile so you guys don't usually suit up. But when you've been

116

with me you have. I'm not at the fertile part of my cycle. So is it a thing? Like you don't want to be naked in me? Or what?"

It was like a bad dream where she was saying all this stuff and had no ability to stop herself. She finally put her hand over her mouth to stop.

She was mortified because, hello, that was not the time and place. Wolves all over the place and they probably heard.

She gathered her tattered self-control and faced him again. "This is not my first case and I don't know what's wrong with me. I don't...I'm not prone to being jealous and saying stuff that is entirely inappropriate for the setting. I'm sorry. I'm so embarrassed." She turned, her face in her hands.

He came to her, enfolding her, his front to her back. Given the very hard cock at her ass, he wasn't upset with her at all.

"It's all right. There's nothing to be embarrassed about. In fact, suffice it to say seeing you jealous and off balance actually makes me hot. Can we make this call to Owen and let them know what's going on, and then you and I can go and talk? I'll explain everything, I promise. Will you trust me enough to do that?" He kissed her temple and she leaned back against him.

"They all heard me. I wish a hole would swallow me up."

He chuckled softly. "Beautiful, wolves are passionate. There's lots of this stuff. All the time. I promise once we talk you'll understand more."

She dragged in a breath and agreed.

They made the call. In Seattle, Gage and Lark were both on it, along with Meriel Owen and her husband Dominic, who ran the Owen Clan of witches.

They were fairly tight lipped, but they did indicate they believed there was something larger at work. Some big bad they didn't know a whole lot about but were looking into. They urged

Rhonda and Gina to teach Michelle some healing and defensive spells and told them to introduce her to Cesare, one of the Portland witches who was apparently a whiz at battle spells. Which should help with her police work.

It was clear the witches in Seattle had an overflowing plate of trouble and they had to deal with this on their own. Which worried Michelle as she tried to imagine what would be worse than that spell she'd felt at the jail.

Things just kept getting worse. Darker and more overwhelming. Which, she supposed, helped her keep in perspective that she'd sort of acted like a jealous dick earlier within the supernatural hearing range of a house full of wolves.

Still, she kept her gaze averted as she ended the call. All around her there was conversation as she gathered her things. Gina hugged her and told her not to worry, Rhonda followed, whispering for Michelle to keep in touch.

They headed toward the front door as she fought a blush and met Tracy, Gabe and Nick's eyes, thanking them for their help and support.

Tracy hugged her and spoke quietly. "Please don't be embarrassed. It's okay. I promise you."

She mumbled more thanks as they left, Josh's hand at the small of her back, guiding her to his car. They both remained quiet as he pulled away and headed back to his place.

Finally, once they'd been in the car a few minutes, Josh cleared his throat to speak, but before he could say anything, her phone rang and it was Dexter.

She blew out a long breath before she answered. "Slattery."

"I'm going to overlook that little temper tantrum you threw earlier. HR tells me you put in for vacation?"

"Yes, sir. I have plenty coming."

"I told you to leave this mess alone."

"With all due respect, sir, it's only been a few days. There is no reason to give up. Especially when I'm taking vacation time and not using department resources."

"*You're* a department resource. Chances are she's run off with one of them. She'll come back when she's done, or when he dumps her."

"You don't know her at all. She would never, ever do that. And if your prejudice didn't color your judgment here, you'd know that. The scene does not point to a woman who ran off with a lover. Her wallet and identification were left behind. Her bank account has been untouched. She left her phone behind. She did not leave of her own accord and there is no way she would have left without telling her mother, her job or me. She's totally responsible. She'd never leave her patients. She's not the person you've decided she is in your head. I've known her my entire life and I will not abandon her when she needs me the most."

Josh put a hand on her knee. Comfort radiated through her system.

"You're walking a dangerous line here, Slattery. Insubordination looks bad on your record. We need you back here. You need to return. Or don't bother."

"Are you threatening to fire me for taking vacation?" Thank heavens for her union which would fight that one big time.

"I'm saying you need to report back here and we can talk about our staffing needs and you can take vacation after we take care of that detail."

All this nonsense simply because he wanted to control her! Hated Others so much that he was fine ignoring reality to bring her back and show her who held her leash.

"I filed my vacation like anyone else. I have the time. I'm taking it. If you wish to attempt the process of termination, you know who my union rep is. Now, as I'm officially on vacation, I'll be hanging up. Sir." And she did before she said anything else.

Normally she would have had to file papers to take vacation in advance. But when she'd called earlier, she'd checked and they'd given her an okay to take the time. Technically she had not broken any rules. And he was a bigoted asshole.

She made a quick call to her union rep and filled him in on the whole mess. He told her not to worry, that he'd handle it if and when Dexter made a move and would be in touch if that happened.

Josh pulled into his parking spot and turned to her.

"What can I do to help?"

"You're doing it. I just..."

"Do you need to go back? Be honest."

"I'm not going back. I'm not a dog on a leash. He's out of line, and I don't want that job if the reality means I'd ignore evidence because of my own prejudicial thinking. I'm not leaving until I find her. It hasn't been that long, damn it."

He pulled her into a hug and she held on tight.

"Come inside and let's talk."

Once they got inside he directed her to go change her clothes, which she had no argument with. She bundled into yoga pants and a sweatshirt with fluffy socks and left her hair in the braid she'd put it in after her shower earlier.

Back in the living room, he pressed a warm mug into her hands. "Tea with whiskey. Sit."

She did and he followed, pulling her close. "I really wanted a different situation to talk to you about all this. You're so stressed and it's been such a horrible time."

"Not knowing whatever it is just makes it worse. Be honest. I may not like it, but damn it, there are too many things I don't know right now and it sucks." She took a sip and hissed.

"Dude, you sure didn't hold back with the liquor." But the warmth that spread through her was welcome so she took another sip and braced herself for whatever it was he was about to spill.

"I'm going to be detailed because I don't know what you do and don't know. So don't be offended if I tell you things you already know."

Michelle made one of those *get on with it* moves with her hand and he snorted a laugh.

"I don't use condoms usually, no. I don't because like you said, we don't pass STDs and we can scent a female's fertility." He was so mad at Esme for that afternoon. She'd heard about his finding a mate because wolves were horrible gossips about that stuff, and when she'd learned he was at Tracy's, she'd come to get a load of Michelle. Stupid.

It had pushed his timeline up and at a time when Michelle really didn't need any added stress.

But it was what it was and he had to deal with it.

"Normally, aside from being messy, it's not a big deal to have unprotected sex with another female. I generally don't...haven't sought out non-shifter females. As you pointed out before, it's too hard to hide what you are. My life is wrapped up with my pack and other wolves. Anyway."

"Oh my God, just say it. You're killing me!"

The whiskey, which he'd added pretty liberally, had kicked in, and he tried not to smile at what a lightweight she was. Then again, he wasn't able to get drunk without a lot of liquor so he might have given her a whole lot. Oops.

"Wolves mate for life. Werewolves too. It's not so much like there is only one person on the entire planet, but it's a rare thing to find that one person. When the male comes inside that female that starts the chain reaction that creates the mate bond. It's magick of its own. It changes the DNA of the female.

The bond between the mated couple is intense. They can feel the emotions of the other. There's no one else after that. Neither mate would want it. For a wolf it's a joy to find."

He swallowed hard.

"I used condoms with you because you're my mate."

She blinked several times and gulped more of her tea before sitting up and putting the mug down. "What?" She stood and began to pace. "You used a condom because you didn't want this supposed joy with me? You wanted it with the other one from Tracy's house? Because I'm not a wolf is that it?"

He jumped up and moved to her. "No." He took her upper arms to halt her in her tracks. "I wanted it from the first moment we hugged in that elevator and I breathed you in. When I tasted you when we kissed that first time. But you're under so much stress and pressure, and I didn't want to spring it on you. I wanted to wait until this thing had settled. Until I'd had some time to woo you a little. I'm messing this up but I want you. So much I don't even know how to put it into words. That after these years, my mate comes into my life and it's someone I've known for so long and already loved?" He tipped her chin up and brushed his lips over hers. "You're my mate. And it *is* a joy.

"And in the interests of full disclosure, when the bond is created there's a need for an anchor bond. For us, wolves I mean, it's part of the process, but you're not a wolf so it's not something you'd have grown up with, or even know about. An anchor is like the third leg on a stool. The power of the bond between a mate pair is such that should one die it could drag the other into death or a mental break they couldn't come back from. So for as long as our history has been passed down, we've had the tri-bond."

"Which is?"

"After the two seal their bond, within two days it's necessary for the female in the pair to have a sort of mating bond with another single male of equal or higher rank to the male in the pair."

Her brows flew up. He knew how it sounded to outsiders, but he wanted, no he needed her to understand at least on some level how important and honored a situation it was.

"Every mated pair does it their own way. Sometimes all three people are there. Other times it's just the female and the anchor. The anchor holds an important place in the lives of that couple. Not a romantic place," he amended quickly. "I know you saw Tracy and Nick and Gabe and you might wonder. But what they have is exceptionally rare. Most of the time the anchor is like a best friend to the couple. A godfather to their kids. He comes to Thanksgiving and Christmas and the big holidays. And when that anchor mates himself, it's generally hoped that the bonded pair opens up their family to the new mate. I know it's a lot. Like I said, I've been wanting to tell you all this at a better time."

"So I'd have sex with another dude. And you'd be down with that?"

"Admittedly, the idea is difficult to imagine now that it's a reality. I've always held it to be a respected tradition and I see it all the time. It works. And it would protect you, which means everything. I know it's shocking and maybe, most likely, outside of what you'd think was okay sexually. But it's a beautiful thing and I'd be with you during the whole thing."

Chapter Nine

"I don't even know what to say."

"I'm sorry this has to be sprung on you like this. I wanted to wait at least a few weeks before I told you. I know you have a lot going on in your head. A lot of stress and pressure. You're it for me. I want you any way I can have you. Nothing has changed. Take the time you need to think on it."

He knew deep down that she wasn't going anywhere. When he'd seen her face as Esme had been touching him, the way she reacted had made his wolf preen. She was pissed off. A pissed-off woman was a magnificent thing to behold. At a distance sometimes. But her being jealous that way meant she felt it too.

Esme had understood it right then and had apologized before she left. Tracy had only smiled and patted his shoulder while telling him they'd work it out.

He'd tell Michelle all that. One day. In months or maybe a year.

Michelle licked her lips, absolutely floored by what he'd said. "I'm pretty sure that test you take for stress factors, you know the one, like moving or getting married or divorced adds points? I'm pretty sure this last week has killed that test dead."

He let go of her upper arms and ran the backs of his fingers against her cheek. She leaned into his touch and felt better. The barest, rawest truth was that when she was with him she was not alone. When she'd been with Gina and Rhonda and they'd used magick and had shown her some things to defend herself, when Owen had hooked her up with the guy who'd teach her defensive and battle magicks, she hadn't been alone.

There was a whole world there in Portland just waiting for her to be part of. A world where she didn't have to be lonely. A world with a man who loved her and wanted to be with her for always. And she didn't doubt what he'd told her. She knew enough to understand the mating stuff. The extra-guy thing was a little unexpected. But...well, it could be okay if she had a choice. Even hot maybe.

"I grew up in a house without a dad. My mom, well, she had a series of boyfriends because she has no real identity unless she's with someone. But her choices, my God. I guess, when I realized it was because she hated herself, hated her magick and that she was a witch so she punished herself with men who weren't good enough for her, I realized that *I* would never let myself be ashamed of that part of myself."

She moved to his windows and looked out over evening in Portland. Wet from rain, the lights glittering, the asphalt dark and slick. He joined her, but didn't get so close she couldn't think.

"So I had this career. And I love being a cop. I'd want to do that here too. Something along those lines. It's part of who I am. I like protecting people. Which I suppose is what you do too, which is pretty cool. Anyway. I am not ashamed of being a witch, but even though I've known it forever and have had contact with other witches pretty much my whole life, I have not really lived as a witch. I think you know more about it than I do."

She wanted to give him the words because he'd been so good to her.

"When I first heard you say I was your mate, I was so angry. I felt rejected." She turned to him, putting her fingers over his lips and then pulled away because every time she touched him she wanted him and she needed to get all this out.

125

"I get it now. I understand, and I'm so grateful you gave me this space even though I'm sure it's been hard. But you did it for me and that means something.

"I've been alone for a long time. I've had Allie and she's important to me. She's my best friend. The only other person I know, before you came back into my life anyway, who shared this secret, who I really could talk to and share with. I never allowed myself to imagine what it would be like to have someone like you. To have something like a mate bond."

She wiped away her tears, and he took her hand, kissing her fingertips.

"I have been so lonely, and you, this world has filled me up in ways I've never thought possible. Suddenly my future is full of so much energy and magick and connection, and I'm thrilled and excited."

He moved to a box of tissues and brought them to her.

"It's immense. There's so much I need to process. And I can't until I find Allie. I'm not rejecting you, but I want to celebrate this thing between us. I want to know more before I do it, and I just can't put that sort of energy into it right now. Do you understand?"

He nodded and kissed her cheeks, so gently that it made her tear up again.

"I'm here. I'm not going anywhere. Take the time you need. I've already told you I'll answer all your questions. Thank you for sharing all that with me. It breaks my heart that you've been so alone and that I contributed to that when I left."

She shook her head and smiled. "I've forgiven that. You've apologized but I get it. I understand why it had to happen, and to be honest with you, I think it was part of the whole big plan anyway. That you and I had our path to walk, had experiences we needed to go through and get past so we could come back together later on and truly appreciate what we had."

"I like that. Tracy said something similar to me. They know. You should hear that from me too. Esme, the female from today..."

She growled. "Her."

He hid a grin but she saw it anyway. "Anyway, wolves are notorious gossips. Once members of the pack see us together, they're going to know. It's all right. We have our own timeline and no one else has a say over it. But I didn't want you going into some event without knowing that."

"I need a soak in some Epsom salts before you get what that look on your face is asking for."

He burst out laughing and sobered quickly. "I'm sorry I hurt you."

"I'm gonna guess it's like anything else. Lots of practice will make me more, um, used to such activity."

He pulled her into a hug, and she held on, her ear pressed to his chest, listening to the steady beat of his heart.

"I do actually have some Epsom salts. Like I said, we heal fast but not instantly."

"I hate that your job is dangerous."

"Ditto, gorgeous. But it's who we are."

"All right. I'm going to make some calls. Just to check in with Pam and this Cesare guy that Gage spoke of. Then I'm going to take a bath and then you can pleasure me."

He snorted. "I'll run you a bath. I have some calls of my own to handle. Some folks from National will be in town next week, and I want to be sure everything is in place."

"I'd have a choice, right? In who the anchor was? Is. Whatever."

"Of course. I mean there are some limits. It has to be a single male who isn't already an anchor, and it has to be someone of my rank or higher. That limits the pool a little. I'm second. It would have to be an Enforcer or something like that, or an Alpha."

She nodded. "All right. As for your work? I've told you, do your job. I'm going to feel bad if you're here instead of doing your work."

"I have all the stuff I need on my computer. I'm connected remotely to our work servers. It's not anything I can't do from here. Damon is handling all the stuff that is pressing at work. By the way, it seems like you and Gina are getting on. She's sort of scary."

"I like her. And Rhonda. I think I can make a life in Portland. With you. And with the witches here. It's nice that she understands the situation that I'll be in as a witch with a Were mate. She's funny and open and I enjoy her. And yes, she's definitely scary."

He went off to start the bath and she checked in. Nothing new with Pam, though the police were on alert after the murder that day. Stricter security protocols in place had slowed everything down, but that was to be expected. Anything Charlie could have told them was now gone. Though certainly he must have known something or they wouldn't have killed him.

He'd been pretty itinerant but some witches and wolves had gone over the camper he lived in, as well as the cops. They found nothing important.

She was so frustrated. Despite the wonder of having a mate and all that, she was desperate to find Allie. Here Michelle had a mate, had a future filled with so much hope, and Allie was out there somewhere alone. Alone and most likely scared. In pain.

Michelle had never in her life felt as helpless as she did right then. She had no idea what else to do. Josh had sent more wolves out that day to scour out even farther from the huge amount of land they'd searched already. They had Allie's scent and the scent of the mages and they found nothing.

She blew out a breath and headed to the bathroom. It was steamy. He'd lit some candles, and she smiled at the sight of a robe he'd laid out for her.

The water was hot, but she slowly slid into it, adjusting bit by bit as the salts did their job, easing the soreness from all parts of her.

She closed her eyes and ran through everything she could. Every piece of evidence, the timeline she knew, all possibilities she could imagine. Maybe if she just went over it she'd think of something new.

He found her drying off and paused to watch her move. The steam carried her scent and his wolf liked that just fine. He felt so much better after talking with her, though he knew she was tortured over her inability to find Allie. Things between them, aside from all the rest, were settled, and he could relax about that at least.

For the time being. Eventually his wolf was going to push a lot harder to claim her. Each minute he was around her, the primal need to seal that bond was a greater weight on him. For now he was all right. Manageable. Barely. But soon enough it would be impossible to be around her, especially when she was upset or in danger, without the bond.

He put all that out of his head as she looked up. "Hey."

"Hey yourself. You feeling better?"

"Physically, yes, I am. The rest? I ran through everything that has happened since I got the call that she was missing. I don't think I've overlooked anything." She shook her head. "I know she's out there alone and I need to find her. I asked Gina and Rhonda as well as Lark and Gage if there were any spells to use to find her. I don't have any of her blood." She swallowed hard. "And I guess I'm glad of that, but at the same time it limits my ability to find her. Maybe."

He leaned there against the doorjamb and watched her process. He hated how upset she was. "I understand, you know? It's the nature of our jobs to have these experiences and frustrations. But when it's someone you care about, it's a million times worse. All the stuff you tell yourself on a regular case, that you're doing everything you can, that sometimes you just can't make it work, well it's not comforting."

She nodded, turning to brush her teeth.

He loved the sight of her in his space. Standing naked at the sink, doing something as mundane as brushing her teeth, but damn it, she marked his life with her presence and it was good. Even with the heartache it was good.

She pulled on the robe, and he allowed himself to move to her to hug her, kissing the top of her head. "You're doing all you can. She's lucky to have you. She knows that."

"If she's still alive. And terrified. Waiting for me to save her and I haven't." She pulled back and padded out to his living room. "I called her mother. She's out of her mind with the waiting and not knowing. Thinking of every horrible scenario. She trusts me to find Allie."

She flopped into the big overstuffed chair near the fireplace he'd turned on while she was in the bath, not wanting her to get cold.

"I told her I was doing all I could. But the words sounded so empty." She slammed a hand against the chair arm, frustrated. "Why can't I find her? I hate just sitting around. I need to be out there doing something. Here I am having so much good stuff in my life. You. Connecting with other witches. I'm smiling and having meals and sleeping. And she is out there." Her voice broke.

He got to his knees before her, taking her hands, his fingers tangling with hers. His wolf needed to comfort her. It made him crazy to see her so upset. If there was anything he could do to fix it, he would. But there wasn't.

"What is it you can do? You went through it all in the bathtub like you said. You could go stand out in the parking lot at the gas station or at the park yet again, and then what? We searched. You were there, Pam was there, I was there, Damon was there. We combed over that whole area and found little more than nothing. I sent my people out and they didn't find anything either. And you've followed up on everything. Sometimes waiting is part of this game. You know that. You're doing all you can to find her."

"She's alone and she's counting on me. I'm fucking up!"

He pulled her close, the scent of her filling him until it nearly hurt.

"You're *not* fucking up. You aren't. But you aren't a superhero either. We keep looking. We do what we can. We know that most likely they took her elsewhere. Not to the stand of park and forest we were in. So tomorrow when it's light, how about we continue down that road we were on? We followed it for a while and found nothing, let's go even farther, maybe take some of the side roads. There are some islands out that way. We'll check those too. We aren't giving up, Michelle. *You* aren't giving up."

Desire rushed over his skin, but he pushed it away. She needed comfort and that's what he'd give her. He kissed the hands he held in his own.

"We're in this together. You're strong. You're smart. You're magnificent."

She smiled through her frustrated tears, and he kissed her cheeks, tasting her pain and upset. Taking that into himself and giving her back love.

She turned into his touch and her lips met his and he took her mouth. Slowly, surely. She was his. He knew it. She'd agreed and certainly he was hers. There was no need to rush. Just learn and be with one another. He didn't know what the next days would hold for Allie. But he knew Michelle would be with him either way.

His wolf seemed to find that satisfactory and eased back a little.

She slid her hands up his chest and to his throat. Her hands strong but so very soft, warm as her thumbs caressed the hollow at the base and then up to his jaw as he continued to kiss her.

"Thank you," she murmured when he broke the kiss.

"For what?"

"For being here for me. For being so supportive. For talking me off the ledge. For opening the door into this life I could never have imagined. I'd have fallen apart if you hadn't been helping me with this."

He shook his head. "No you wouldn't have. You'd be muddling through because that's who you are. But I'm so glad I've been here with you. So glad the witch whose delightful ass I was checking out turned out to be you."

"You checked out my ass?"

He snorted. "Is that a question? I came into the lobby and there was this woman there with the nicest ass. I checked you out before you'd even turned around. That it was attached to you, and that you're my mate? Well that's cake."

"I'm sort of drunk. You put a lot of liquor in that tea. I figured I'd sweated it out in the bath."

"How about I order in and we watch a movie? You haven't eaten in hours, and you should know wolves need to eat about every three hours to keep up with our metabolisms. Though...do you get horny when you're drunk?"

She rolled her eyes. "It seems that I'm permanently horny when I'm in your general proximity. It's sort of disconcerting."

"Not for me." He shrugged and stood.

A ringing phone woke her up just after dawn, three days after he'd revealed to her that she was his mate. Josh was already up, moving around. Probably in his office playing catch up on his own work as he'd been spending so much time away from it, driving Michelle all over the city looking for that SUV or for signs, any signs, of Allie. They'd even headed up to Seattle, stopping at all the rest stops north and south on the way back for any signs of the mages, and found nothing.

Guilt flashed through her again. Sure he'd told her he had things in hand, but she felt bad for taking him away from the office.

Rolling from bed and sliding into the robe, she moved to the bathroom to brush her teeth, the muffled sound as he answered and spoke to whoever rumbled in the background.

And then she paused, a chill running through her at the change in his tone.

She rushed out and down the hall as he was writing something down. "Yes, yes. On the way. I need to wake her up. Yes, I know. I'll rush. Try to hold off calling anyone else until we arrive."

He hung up and turned, he was so pale she knew it was bad.

"What?"

"Get dressed. One of the teams of wolves I sent out stumbled on a house with the scent of the mages. And something else. Pam is there, she's holding things down until we arrive. Damon is on the way as well."

"What is it? You're pale."

"They smell death inside. It doesn't necessarily mean it's her. Just, let's get out there now."

With trembling hands she got dressed before rushing into the bathroom to brush her teeth. She pulled her hair into a ponytail in the car on the way to the scene, trying really hard not to think about it. Hoping that the scent of death was anyone but Allie.

He parked on the side of the road and turned to her. "We're not going to get any closer in the car. I don't want any evidence of our presence that close. Not until we know more."

She got out, and they jogged down a street and then up a dirt road. "It's a mile or so up here, Pam says."

Michelle got caught in a web of despair about five minutes later as the house came into view on a vista just ahead.

"Yes, they've been here." She tried not to gag on the fetid, rotten-meat stench of that magic they used. Wrong energies. Dark.

Pam was waiting for them, along with Damon and one of the wolves she remembered from the lobby that first day she'd come to ask for Pacific's help.

"We haven't gone in yet." Pam looked to Josh and then to Michelle. "You ready? You go low, I'll go high."

Michelle had worn her vest and she was glad. And she hoped the spell she'd learned the day before from Gina to defend herself would work.

The closer they got, the worse the stench was. From the faces on the Weres all around her, it wasn't just a magical stench but a physical one. And then she smelled it, death. Not just death magics, but the smells that indicated someone had died and died badly. Still fresh enough that it probably had been within the last eight or so hours.

Josh kicked the door in so hard it flew off the hinges, and as they'd planned, Pam went high and left while Michelle kept low and went right.

They swept through room by room. The house only had four rooms, and so when they found nothing, they went out the back door and that's when she saw it.

Michelle made a sound. She didn't know where it had come from, only that it was full of everything she'd been feeling. All her grief and guilt and fear. A sound that ripped from her so hard it hurt.

Allie lay, bloodied and broken in the center of a circle. A blood circle, not a salt circle.

"Wait!" She held up a hand as she dug through the pocket of her jacket and pulled out a bag of salt she'd blessed only the day before according to Lark's directions.

She spoke softly, through tears as she traced another circle just inside the blood circle. She tried hard not to look at Allie as she did.

No birds sang. There was no sound in that yard and there should have been. The leaves on the trees should have been rustling. There should have been insect sounds, the rustle of small things in the underbrush. But there was nothing.

Once she finished the circle, she spoke the last words of the spell, and the power rushed through her and broke the blood circle with a rush of sticky, sick energy that thankfully disappeared quickly.

What didn't dissipate though, was the stench of death.

Michelle broke the salt circle. She moved to Allie. Pam approached and put a hand on her shoulder. "This is a crime scene. Remember that."

It wasn't like she needed to check a pulse.

There was nothing left in Allie. Her magick, her aura usually so vibrant in Michelle's othersight, was gone. There was *nothing*. She'd moved on. She'd been brutalized. Left torn, broken and empty on the ground like garbage.

"I have to call this in. I need all the wolves gone. Michelle, you can stay. But we can't touch anything else."

"Before they get here, I'm going through the house one more time to get scents." Damon paused and then took Michelle's hand. "I'm sorry, Michelle. We will find justice for this. I promise you."

She nodded, absently. "Is Gina being protected?"

His expression turned feral. "Yes. At all times."

Josh watched, saying nothing until Pam stepped away to call it in and get crime-scene folks out.

He took Michelle's hand, drawing his thumb back and forth across her skin. She stiffened and took her hand back.

"God, beautiful, I'm so sorry. I want to hold you so much. I wish this was different."

She shook her head hard, once. "It's not. I need to deal with this. I can't afford to lose my shit right now. I have to do my job and I can't if you touch me."

He nodded. "I understand. I don't like the idea of leaving you here."

"You have to. I can't explain you to the cops. Pam is under enough scrutiny right now. You have to go. But if you'd have my car brought over, I'd appreciate it."

"That I can do." He paused. "I love you, Michelle. You're not alone. No matter what."

She turned, catching his gaze, and that connection between them clicked into place. She nodded, shoving back all her emotions. She needed to be cold and hard and ruthless right then. She needed to examine that scene with every single one of her senses, and that meant she had no room for guilt, or even love.

Chapter Ten

She pulled up to her apartment and sat in the car for long minutes, unable to bring herself to even move.

Back in Portland, she'd stayed at the scene while it had been processed. They canvassed the neighborhood, but the houses were very far apart so no one claimed to have seen anything. The place they'd found Allie in was supposed to have been empty, the last tenants having left six months before. No one had noticed anything at all.

She searched for the mage energy all around, driving aimlessly after she'd left the scene, but saw nothing.

In the end, nearly on autopilot, she'd gotten on the freeway and headed south. She couldn't inform Kathy of her child's death by phone, and she sure as hell didn't trust Dexter to send anyone over there who'd gently break the news.

So she'd gone straight to Kathy's once she'd gotten off the freeway. Luckily Allie's aunt had been there, but still, she'd had to tell a mother that her child was dead. Even with a judicious removal of detail, it was hard to say and even harder for Kathy to hear.

They'd all cried for what seemed like hours, and still, she'd held back a great deal of her grief because she didn't want any more of a burden on Kathy. Allie's aunt was able to get Kathy to rest, and though she'd offered a place for Michelle to stay, she'd refused and driven around town for some time before she'd ended up home.

Her phone rang and she saw Josh's number. Immediately she felt better.

"Hey."

"Hey yourself, beautiful. Where are you?"

She'd called him halfway to Roseburg to let him know what she was doing. He'd been angry that she'd gone without him, but she'd simply explained Kathy had a right to know as soon as possible and she needed to hear it directly from someone who loved Allie too.

And she needed that time in the car, all by herself, to process—or try to process—all she'd been through in the last week. The time to feel whatever the hell she wanted to without worrying over how anyone else would react.

"I'm getting out of my car now. I'm at my apartment. I've been at Kathy's for the last four hours." Exhaustion dogged her steps as she headed down the path to her place. The air was clean and crisp. She should have been cold but she just didn't feel much of anything.

"I'll be back up soon. Kathy has to make funeral arrangements. They'll release the body in a day or two." Not like it wasn't clear Allie had been torn to pieces, but she understood the authorities wanted to get as many details as they could before they let the family have the body for burial.

"I won't ask how you are. I can hear it. Damn it, Michelle, I wish you hadn't gone down without me."

She unlocked her door and turned off her alarm. She might have been tired, but not too tired to use her othersight to be sure no one else had been in her place or was there now. Relieved that she was alone and everything was undisturbed, she locked up and slumped down the hall. Noting her bed was still messy from where she'd jumped up just a week earlier when Kathy had called to say Allie was missing.

Had it only been seven days?

Josh was speaking and she realized she hadn't heard a word.

"I'm sorry. I was using my othersight, I didn't hear you."

He sighed and she knew he worried. She knew he ached to help and make her better. It meant something. Everything really. No one had been that to her before. Not in the way he was. "Everything is safe? *You're* safe?"

Physically? Sure. It was emotionally and mentally she wasn't so sure of. "Yes. No one's been here."

"Give me your address, just so I have it, and go to sleep if you can."

She did. And then she hesitated and realized she needed to say something before she lost her nerve. "Josh?"

"Yes, beautiful?"

"I love you."

His breath caught. "Sweetheart." So much emotion in one word. It had to be hard for him, the protective alpha wolf that he was, to be away from her. All of that longing rang in his tone. "I love you too. Lock your doors. Get some rest. I'll talk with you soon."

She managed to stumble into the shower to wash the stink of death off. But it wasn't gone from her heart. Now that no one depended on her, she let it go. Let the walls holding back all the emotion fall. The tears came in hot, gut-wrenching sobs as she shook so hard she could barely keep her feet.

She'd failed. The most important task she'd ever had and she'd failed. And the cost was higher than she could bear. She'd never hear Allie laugh again. Never go bowling with her or innertube down the river. They'd never again go shoe shopping and bitch about men together. Michelle would never be able to tell her about Josh coming back into her life in such an improbable way.

Her best friend had died alone and terrified. And for what? In truth, Allie hadn't even been that gifted a witch! A little bit of power, most of it for healing and nurturing. And now she'd never get married and have babies. She'd never finish another one of Michelle's sentences.

There were no words to describe how bereft Michelle was left after that loss. It seemed unbelievable that Allie simply did not exist anywhere in the world anymore. Last weekend they'd gone to the outlet malls and goofed around looking for handbags, and now she was dead.

Stupid. Horrible.

Senseless. *Damn it.*

The water had long since run cold and shivers wracked her body when she finally came back to herself. There were no tears left.

She got out, not bothering with anything more than a cursory rub with a towel, and then fell into bed.

If she hadn't been so damned drained from all the grief and guilt, she might have been kept up, tormented by the images of that day. Instead she fell hard and fast into the kind of sleep blessedly free of dreams. But she was dimly aware, as she slipped into sleep, that Josh wasn't next to her and she'd gotten used to him so fast.

Josh had called her as he left Portland, but once he'd heard her voice he knew she needed sleep more than he needed to see her. He could wait.

A few hours at least.

After he got to Roseburg, he allowed himself a cruise down the street he'd grown up on. Where he'd ridden his bike and his skateboard. His parents had moved to Colorado a few years before. He'd never visited, though his mother had issued a few halfhearted invitations.

He wished he had feelings about it. But all he had was ambivalence. In the ten years since he'd gone off to college, he'd seen them twice. Once at a funeral of one of his paternal grandparents. He'd had cake and drank bad coffee from a church urn and had left after an hour at the wake. And then once before they'd gone to Colorado. He'd met them at the airport, and they'd had lunch at a crappy hotel diner while they waited for their flight.

He didn't miss them. Didn't think to call them when something good happened in his life. Didn't give much thought to them one way or the other. And he didn't think they did of him really either.

He had a family. Not one he was born to. But one he'd made. A group of people who'd proven to him over and over that they would always have his back. And now he had Michelle.

He drove to her apartment complex and parked, taking a walk through the grounds as the sun rose. Making sure she was safe. Giving himself something to do instead of going to her door.

He'd left her the day before at the scene of that horrible murder. It had been hard to do, though he understood the reasons for it. He'd had to walk away and trust Pam to take care of her in his absence. Yes, yes, Michelle was a cop, she saw rough things, but none of the victims had been her best friend before.

And she'd been there hours. Helping with the canvass of the neighborhood, Pam had said. And then she'd gotten in her car and headed to Roseburg. Without him.

She'd called him to let him know and he'd been so angry. Hurt. But then he'd let it go because he understood it. Understood that she needed him, but was giving that up so she could go be there for Kathy, not trusting anyone else to tell her about Allie with as much kindness and compassion as Michelle could. Needing to grieve with someone who loved Allie too.

So he'd tied up his loose ends and had packed a bag and headed to her. The longer they were separated, the more antsy he was.

What he hadn't expected was the way his wolf had risen and refused to back down. He *needed* to claim her. Being separated when she was in such an emotional state had pushed him to the breaking point. The wolf had let the man handle it for a week, but now it was time to let the man know he wasn't human and his mate was unclaimed.

Claimed, he could protect her better. Claimed, he'd have a tie to her that would enable him to soothe, comfort and defend. He knew she'd had a lot to manage in the last week. Knew the bond would add more to that list. And yet, he also knew the thing between them was real. Knew the bond would make things better. Not totally, she had a lot of grieving in her future, he understood that too.

After he'd prowled the grounds and before the cops got called due to a man hanging around the area, he headed back to his car to wait for her to wake up. He wanted her to get as much rest as she could.

He did some work and tried to not look up every two minutes toward the building where her apartment was. And like magick—he supposed it was magick of sorts—he knew when she'd woken up. Even without the bond he knew it. He got out and walked to her door, knocking after he'd taken a deep breath to try to gain some control.

She shuffled into her kitchen and started a pot of coffee. She'd need to call Josh in a bit, let him know she was awake and also that she'd missed him. Just hearing his voice would make her feel better.

Being back in Roseburg, even after that short time in Portland, had made everything far more clear. Now that Allie was gone, she had nothing holding her in town and everything beckoning her to Portland.

What she had now, well it wasn't logical really, though she had known him a very long time. She could tell herself it couldn't possibly be love. And she could tell herself that in the face of the knowledge that she did love him. But what would be served?

Allie would have told her to shut up and accept it like the gift it was. Sometimes you just *knew* things. Another thing she knew was that his wolf chafed at the inability to claim her. Gina had broken down and told her how difficult it was for any male to not seal a mate bond, especially when they were living with and having sex and intimacy with their mate. She didn't want that for him. Not any longer. She wanted him to be able to take that step with her.

They'd talk about it when she got back to Portland.

She peeked into her fridge and pulled out a yogurt and then heard the knock on her door. With a sigh, she headed over. She'd slept in her sweats and a T-shirt so she was relatively decent.

One look through the peephole had her turning off the alarm and yanking the door open to find Josh on her doorstep. Joy filled her at the sight of him.

She smiled but then noted his eyes. Holy shit, his wolf was right there at the surface. She'd seen him change, knew that look.

"I need you," he said in a low growl.

She knew without a doubt that if she let him in he'd claim her right then and there. There was no turning back from this moment. If she said no, he'd go and eventually find someone else.

But she didn't want that. She wanted to be his all the way. Damn everything else. This was a gift and she had no intention of letting that go.

She stepped aside, and he came in, kicking the door closed, locking it and pulling the security chain. She set the alarm again, her gaze not leaving him as he circled her like prey.

"I'd ask if you were okay but I know you're not. And I'm sorry. Sorry for all you've lost."

"You came to me."

He stepped close and pulled her to him, his arms sliding around her and making her feel as if she'd truly come home. Her body to his, his scent in her nose, his heartbeat against her cheek.

"I will always come to you. Always. Do you accept that? Accept me and what I am? What *we* are? I know I said I'd wait as long as you needed, but holy shit I need you so much right now it's sort of scary. My wolf is out of patience."

She smiled and pulled back, taking his hand and leading him to her bedroom, turning off the coffeemaker as she passed.

He paused and took a deep breath once he'd entered the room. "Smells like you in here."

She smiled. "I should hope so. Now it'll smell like you too."

He held out a hand and she took it. "Come here. You're all sleep warm. Sad though. I'm sorry." He brushed the hair away from her face.

She shrugged. "You're here. So I'm a little bit less sad."

He pulled her shirt up over her head and hummed, running his hands all over her skin, bending his head to take her mouth. She opened to him immediately, sucking his tongue, delighting in the way he pulled her to him tighter. He kissed down her neck, over her shoulder and then shoved her sweats down so she could step out of them.

When she opened her eyes, he was already on his way to naked, and she frowned a moment before deciding it was okay that she hadn't seen him start to get undressed because that's how she wanted him anyway.

She kissed across his chest, licking over his skin as she got his jeans undone and halfway down his thighs. "Off."

"Impatient."

But she heard his wolf in his voice, and she knew she wasn't the only one impatient.

"In me," she spoke against his mouth as he moved in for another kiss.

"First things first. I'm going to lick your pussy until you come. Get you nice and wet. Relax you a little and then I'm going to fuck you."

She swallowed hard and fisted him, pumping up and down, smearing her thumb through the bead of precome at the slit. She licked it, and he growled, pushing her to her back on the bed, and settled in between her thighs. "Wait on that. I don't want to be right on the edge before I even get inside you naked the first time."

He went straight for her pussy, and she had no complaints, though she didn't have his cock in her hand any longer. She arched, rolling her hips as he slid his tongue up and into her over and over before surging to her clit, moving his tongue and lips back and forth across it, sending her to the edge immediately.

So good. Damn he was so good at this. Fast or slow, he knew her body and did all the things she liked. Did them hard and soft, gently and not so gently, until her climax began to settle in. She dug her heels into the bed, her hips churning

146

against his mouth as she tugged his hair, hard, to keep him exactly there. He hummed, and that vibration was the last little bit she needed before she fell over and orgasm consumed her as he kept devastating her with that mouth of his.

A smaller aftershock orgasm stole through her, leaving her boneless, and then he moved, looming over her, his mouth on hers, her taste on his lips, and it stole her breath.

He brushed the head of his cock against her, through the heated slick of her cunt, and snarled. *So. Good.* With a condom it had been good, but this? This was exquisite sensation. Inferno hot and so wet he slid in, easy at first but then she gripped him tight.

He paused as his heart beat in his cock for long moments. *Throb-throb-throb.* She tightened around him and he shook his head. "Careful there, beautiful. I'm so very close, and I want your cunt around me for a while before I blow."

He thrust all the way in and sloooowly retreated. Over and over as it became nearly hypnotic, that slow and deep fucking. She drew her knees up to his sides, getting him even deeper. He dropped down to lick over her nipples, taking in her taste.

His woman.

His mate.

His.

Her hands roamed over his shoulders, nails digging in, urging him on. The prick of pain shot through him as it did when she lost the veneer on her control and her claws came out.

"I want you to mark me again," she whispered, and he groaned as he skittered even closer to climax at the sound of those words.

He bent his head and licked over the side of her breast. "Here?" He tested his teeth against the firm mound of flesh, and she shivered.

"Yes."

He sucked. Hard enough he knew he'd leave a love bite. And then he bit and she came around his cock so hard he almost lost his mind.

"Someone likes it rough."

"Yeah? Me too." She smiled and arched up, biting his pec, and he growled as sensation surged, speeding his pace as the sharp pain of her teeth tingled into a pleasure so intense he had to get deep, had to come inside her and make her his in every way.

Their sexual interludes had been hot each and every time. But this was more raw than before. His emotion was so close to the skin, as hers was. She wanted it, wanted him, wanted to belong to him in a way she'd never felt before.

He began to fuck into her so hard she bounced a little each time he got in all the way. Her tits swayed and the grin he gave her as he watched was rakish.

She arched, dragging her nails up his sides, delighting in his growl.

"Now, beautiful." And he came so hard she felt it.

And then it was...it filled her. Up and up and up. She felt so much she wasn't sure she could take any more. She would have panicked if he hadn't been there, pulling her into his arms as he rained kisses over her face. Murmuring endearments and soft words as her world was rocked. Literally.

She had to close her eyes against the tilt in her equilibrium as it sucked her under. Emotion rushed through her as she drowned in the way she felt and then the way *he* did. Sounds, scents, everything all around her amped up. Even the bedding beneath her demanded her attention with the cool caress of cotton. It was so much.

Was it supposed to be like this? It was too late to back out, and he didn't seem alarmed so she hoped that meant it was okay. She let it take her, all that sensation, all those demands for sensory attention, and she trusted he'd make sure she'd get through.

She lost herself for a little while, and when she opened her eyes, she had to drag in a breath at the intensity of the connection she had with him.

He pressed a cool cloth against her face and neck. "Are you all right?" She didn't even remember him getting out of bed.

"How long was I...um...whatever that was?"

"A few minutes. You're fine now. I've been told the change, the binding, is a little harder on a non-wolf. You're so beautiful." He kissed her softly.

She swallowed hard and tried to sit up as the world shifted enough that she remained on her back. "This is...are *you* all right?"

He smiled down at her, and the way he felt wasn't just clear in his features, it was like she felt it too. A burst of love. Of adoration. Of the need to protect. Even of the loam and forest of his wolf. All he was when it came to his feelings about her was there and she knew it.

"I'm fucking perfect." He took her hand and put it over his heart. "You're here now. I can feel you, Michelle. You're amazing."

So much emotion. It was perfect and wonderful and beyond anything she'd ever felt, and it was totally and completely okay. She belonged to something bigger and more important than she'd dreamed of. "Incredible. This is...thank you. This is the best thing I've ever felt. And it's all because of you. Wow, this is better than the first spell I ever learned. Better than anything. I love you, Josh. I don't know that I ever stopped, but teenage-girl love has nothing on this. I've decided I'm going with it. Magick, whatever it is. I'm in."

He kissed her again, long and slow. "I love you too." He nipped her bottom lip and she snuggled closer. "Mate."

"I like that. Mate."

"Me too."

When she got out of the shower, he'd made her some breakfast, and coffee waited on the table.

"Wow, you're handy in all sorts of ways."

"I figured you'd need the sustenance. Pam called."

She took the coffee and sat, putting eggs on her plate. She realized his emotions were like a radio station. She could choose to tune in and listen or turn the sound down. He was worried, upset. "Tell me."

"They're not going to release the body for at least a week. There's not a whole lot of it left, and she thinks you should have a talk with Kathy about having the body cremated in Portland and then sent down here. Save her any trauma of seeing Allie in that condition."

She'd had a feeling it would be like that.

"I went over it with her last night. I didn't want to alarm her or give her more detail than she needs. She doesn't need to know all of it. Hell, I wish I didn't know it all. But I did say there was no chance of an open casket for a viewing and I did push for a cremation. She's not going to be pleased about the delay in releasing the body but I get it. They want to see what the hell is going on. That scene, it was like out of a movie. The authorities are going to start talking occult or something like that soon. I called Owen about it. They're dealing with a bunch of stuff right now as well. More disappearances all over the country."

He ate quietly, watching her.

"What?"

"Will you come back with me? To Portland?"

She sucked in a breath. "Yes. I mean, I do need to be around to help Kathy when she needs it. But right now her family is there. I can't go back to work. Dexter said, when I told him, *see what comes of mixing with them*, and I knew right then I had to quit. I'll give my notice but time it so I don't have to go back at all. Save them the trouble of disciplining me, I guess. It'll look better on a job application elsewhere if I didn't get fired."

She felt the hot rush of his anger at that. "Gonna take some getting used to. This connection thing."

"Strong emotions are easiest to feel through the bond. I can't believe he'd be so heartless. It makes me want to punch him in the face."

"Get in line. I don't get it, but I can't waste any more time on trying to get him to see the error of his ways. I know there are some pretty good guys left. I'll speak to them to be sure they keep an eye on Kathy."

"Good idea. Do you think she'd go away for a while? For safety's sake?"

She shook her head. "No way. She has a life here. She won't go. But her sister will stay on a month or two so that will help." She sighed. "I just can't be here right now. She's everywhere and I can't. There's like part of me missing. I keep reaching for it to use it, to pick up the phone and call her to tell her about you, about this, and I can't because she's gone."

He got up and moved to her, pulling her into a hug. Her upset smoothed a little.

"You're like Prozac."

He chuckled. "The bond has a lot of plusses. You have that effect on me too. Still, I wish I could make this better. I wish it ended differently for her. You did all you could. I wish you could see that."

"I wish I could too. Maybe after some time goes by." She suspected she'd feel like a failure over this for the rest of her days. "She's gone and I'm not. If I saw something earlier. If I had tried this or that. I don't know. But she died alone and terrified, and I wasn't there to save her."

His arms tightened around her. "I know. And it kills me for both of your sakes. I believe you did all you could and more. But I know *you* and understand you're going to run it over and over and over until you're convinced you did all you could and maybe that'll never happen for you. I want to shoulder all your burdens but I get that I can't in every case. Now that we're bound, it's like that imperative is turned up to twelve on the dial. I want to sling you over my shoulder and run away with you. Take you somewhere no one can find us. But I also realize that's not going to happen. So we'll have to work it through. Together though. Because that's what has to happen. You need to let me help."

"I know. I'm trying. I guess the anchor thing needs to happen now. Or soon."

He sucked in a breath. "Yes. It should be in the next day or two. There are some wolves coming in from Boston. Late this afternoon, actually. That's why I was asking if you were coming back home with me. Well aside from me wanting you with me in our place. I want to handle the security myself from the airport. Jack Meyers, he's the National Enforcer. He's coming to Portland to meet with Tracy, Nick and Gabe before he heads up to Seattle for a meeting of the packs to talk about this whole mage thing. There'll be a lot of higher-ranked wolves around. Not Jack, he's mated, has a version of a tri-bond actually. But there will be others, unmated wolves."

"Like an assortment of chocolates. Or a buffet. So what if, you know, we end up a threesome? I'm not sure I can handle two alpha males. One is exhausting enough."

He snorted. "It's going to be all right. Like I said, the whole threesome thing is totally rare. Jack is mated with a witch and a jaguar shifter. The witch and the jaguar were together first. They'd imprinted, which is sort of the jaguar version of mating. And then Jack met her and she was his mate. They're all three together and mated. It's intense, but it totally works for them."

"I'm a witch. What if it's some kooky witch thing?"

"We won't get you anywhere near a jaguar." He held back a grin but she felt his amusement anyway.

"Har."

"It's new to you. I know. I'm just teasing. It's going to be fine. Gina is a witch and she's mated to Damon. No threesome, just the two of them."

"Are you anyone's anchor? Gah! Maybe I don't want to know. I guess I have to know because this is like part of your wolf thing. But I have to be friends with some chick you had sex with and you're sort of mated to?" She realized, slightly panicked, that *she* was going to have to sex up a near stranger she'd be bonded to on some level. Did she shave her legs that day?

He kissed her nose. "I'm not, no. And now that I'm mated, it's not ever going to happen, so that's that. As for the tri-bond? I think you should look at this as a hot thing." He slid his thumb over her bottom lip. "Hot sex with someone, sanctioned by your mate."

"Are you going to be there? In the room, I mean?"

"I think yes. I'd go crazy if I wasn't. Is that all right?"

"This is all so weird."

He grinned. "Sit and finish your breakfast. I brought boxes so you can pack up your car and mine, and we can go home. My place is our place now."

"Avoiding the subject?"

"No. But I think you need some time to digest all this, and then when we get to Portland, you can meet more wolves and we can work it out and it won't be as weird. Hopefully. I'm sorry you're uncomfortable. Well, part of me is happy because it means you're not jumping all over having sex with someone else. But I don't want you to be unhappy."

"I'm rolling with it the best I can."

"I know."

Chapter Eleven

He met Jack and the rest of his wolves at the airport. Michelle was heading to his apartment once she got back to town to unpack her things. She'd stopped by Allie's mom's place on her way out of town so he knew she'd need some time on her own to process.

He smiled. Her things in his place. *Their* place now. He'd pick her up when they'd gotten everyone settled in, and they'd go to a pack dinner where she'd be introduced as his mate.

"Congratulations are in order, I hear." Jack grinned his way.

"Thank you. It's a good day to be me. This being-mated thing is pretty sweet. No wonder all you guys walk around smiling all the time."

"It is indeed a good thing. Tell me about her."

"Of all things, she's my high school sweetheart. My first love. I left Roseburg and everyone in it behind when I was bitten. Anyway, she showed up at the offices downtown needing our help, and it turns out she's my mate. And a witch, which I never knew. She's a cop. Beautiful. Brilliant. A badass with some mad skills with a handgun. She's perfect."

"Oh the goofy smile and glazed eyes of the newly mated." Jack laughed. "It's a great story though. One your kids are going to love. Also being a cop means she'll understand your job, which is good."

"And she can defend herself in the face of all this crazy stuff with the mages." Akio Minami, Jack's right hand in his Enforcer crew, spoke from the back seat.

"Yes, that too. This is some shit. This murder scene we found her friend at? I've seen a lot, but what they'd done to this witch? I want to lock her up in my place with fifty guards all armed to the teeth."

Jack growled. His mate was a witch too, so he understood, all too well, the nature of this threat and how it hit so very close to home.

"Cade wanted me to relay how much he'd appreciate it if you'd take Akio out to the scene. We should have as much information shared as possible. We've had our own trouble with the mages out our way, as you know. I want him to compare the scents to see if there are any connections."

Josh nodded as he headed to the old Pacific Pack House where Nick's parents, the retired Alpha pair, still lived. Visiting wolves often stayed there, and big meetings and gatherings were held there.

"We can go out tomorrow if that works. The Joining is tonight." The Joining was the ceremony where a mate was presented to the pack, and if he or she wasn't already a member, they'd be made members after swearing fealty to the Alphas.

Jack was an anchor to Tracy's sister-in-law Grace, the female National Alpha, which made him like family in a very real sense. It was a good thing to have him at the ceremony later that night.

"Yes, that would be fine. Thank you," Akio said.

"How's she on the tri-bond?"

"Nervous. I had to talk her down earlier when she was convinced we'd have a threesome like you and Tracy have."

"Truth be told, it's a nice thing to have another male around to deal with our beautiful but totally headstrong woman. I expect Gabe and Nick feel the same."

"Don't go mentioning any of that around her, thanks."

Jack laughed. "I'm pretty smooth when I want to be, dumbass."

He dropped them off and headed back home to get his mate.

He got home and breathed in deep. Her scent, her magick hung in the air, mixing with his.

She wandered out and smiled at the sight of him, though her eyes were still puffy from all the crying, and that sense of sadness over the loss of her friend still emanated from her. "Everyone get in okay?"

He nodded, moving to her to kiss her. "Everything is much better now that I'm here with you. How is Kathy?"

"Really sedated. She did understand what I said when I told her about the delay in releasing Allie. She's not happy. But Allie's aunt did convince her to have a funeral home up here handle things. They have the number here and my cell. I didn't go into a lot of detail about moving up here, but I mentioned I'd reconnected with you and that we were together."

"What about your mom?"

She made a face but he felt a twinge of her sadness. "I left a voicemail. She's not in town. But I can't imagine she's going to care much one way or the other."

"Her loss. We're family now."

She nodded.

He followed her back to the bedroom where she'd already unpacked several boxes. "You've gotten a great start. Can I help unpack?"

"No, I've got it. I took over the dresser in the other room. Yours is too full."

"I told you to take three of the drawers in here." He frowned.

"You have a lot of clothes, Josh. It's okay. The dresser in the other room was pretty much empty. I did take a few of the drawers in your closet for my underwear. Do I have to dress up for this thing tonight? I mean like cocktail stuff or what?"

"A dress would be good, but not like black tie. We have people in from another pack so it's good to look nice. But you're gorgeous so that's already handled."

She held up two dresses, a bright green one and a red one.

"The green one, definitely."

"It's a bit more low cut than the red. Is that okay?"

He barked a laugh. "Am I okay with your boobs being visible?"

She blushed. "Not all of them! Just my cleavage."

"I'm always okay with cleavage."

She looked over at the clock. "When do we have to be there?"

He took one look and groaned. "We need to leave here in about half an hour."

"Shit!" She grabbed the dress and headed into the bathroom where he could see she'd taken over half the space, and the sink on the left. "You stay back with your sex eyes, mister. I have to get ready and we don't have time for what you're after."

"I can make it good and quick too."

She snorted, rolling her eyes. "You are not a quick type. And I'd have to shower afterward or everyone would know exactly what we were up to before we arrived."

She shucked her clothes, and he leaned back and watched, fingers itching to touch all that skin.

"They're going to assume it anyway."

"I already took a shower. I want to look good for this, Josh. All the females you took for a ride will be there, and I want people to think you made out okay instead of *oh bummer, look what poor Josh bonded with.*"

He moved to her, pulling her in for a long slow kiss. He licked his lips, taking one last taste of her before he stepped away a little.

"You could show up in a garbage bag and they'd still think I was a very lucky wolf. As for those other females? They know who you are and what you are. And that's everything. You understand?"

She gave him a smile. "Yeah, yeah."

He grabbed a quick shower and got dressed as she got ready, putting on makeup and doing her hair in tousled curls around her face.

At least the party thing was stressful enough to give her something else to worry over beside the awful weight of Allie's loss. It was strange to have so much happiness in her life even as at the same time she drowned in crushing, horrible sadness.

She'd spent the hours driving back to Portland alternating between tears and happiness. But he helped. Being around him helped, soothed her. Though she also understood he realized she was in pain and that she had every right to feel like crap because of it.

But life went on and she had to do all this stuff. The tribond thing especially. Gina had talked to her a little about it when she'd called to ask her opinion on what to wear that night. Gina's anchor lived in Portland, and they had dinner with him a least twice a month. He and Damon were good friends. Michelle didn't want to say she thought it was weird. Though she did. But who was she to judge? It was someone else's culture, and she'd have to find her own peace with it because in a big way, it was her culture now too.

So she sucked it up because there was nothing else to do but suck it up and try to move forward.

Tracy came out as they pulled up, the girls practically bouncing at the sight of Josh. When he got out of the car, they clapped and started calling his name. He grinned at them but moved to get Michelle's door first.

"Wow, Michelle, you look great!" Tracy laughed as the girls leapt into Josh's arms. They giggled and kissed his cheeks as Tracy made her way over. "Welcome. To Pacific and to the house and all that. I wanted to tell you how sorry I am about your friend. Anything we can do to help is yours. I know you're starting over up here, so please know you've got a shoulder and an ear whenever you need it. You don't know me well, but I'd like us to be friends. I moved here and didn't know anyone either."

Touched, she nodded. "Thanks, I appreciate it. It's all so much. I feel...I don't know anything. Not just about your world but my own really. I don't want to embarrass Josh or do something wrong."

"Plenty of folks who are happy to share. Just ask and if we can get you the answer we will."

"I'm nervous," Michelle blurted out.

"I know there are a lot of people here, but they're all here to celebrate you. To welcome you. This is something really special to us. The bond, I mean. Josh is so happy. Everyone is going to see that. He leads them, keeps them safe. To see him happy and with his mate is a good thing. My pack will see you as a positive. Even before they meet you, they'll think that."

"Aw, thanks. But I also mean the anchor thing."

Tracy took her hands and squeezed. "That's going to be all right too. I mean." Tracy shrugged and looked around the area, full of ridiculously gorgeous people. "They're all beautiful.

You're beautiful. Josh is hot. Just...it's part of the process. Let it happen. It's your choice, you know."

Tracy walked with her up the steps and into the house. Josh had the hands of both girls as he followed.

"Let's see." Tracy scanned the room. "Ah, so over there, that's Trace. He's here from Cascadia. He's ranked lower than Josh, but his power level is high. High enough to be the Alpha of his own pack anywhere else. He's an Enforcer too, works for my sister, who runs the Enforcer team up there."

Trace had long pale hair tied loosely back from his face. Piercing brown eyes.

"Over there is Erik, he's visiting here from Boston with Jack, that hot blond-surfer-looking dude."

"Jack is the National Enforcer, right? He's also in a threesome and he's anchored to your sister-in-law?"

"You're a fast learner. Yes, that's Jack. Oh and then there's Akio. Akio is Jack's right hand."

Holy cow. Now *that* was a beautiful man in a room full of really exceptional-looking people.

Tracy continued. "The anchor is special. They make a commitment to you to take on the weight of the death of a mate. It's...hard to explain, but it's more than just fucking. Your anchor is part of your family. None of them agrees to do it lightly. We're all a bit superstitious, wolves I mean. We believe in fate and all that jazz. So just because an available wolf is around, he may not agree to serve as an anchor. There has to be chemistry. He has to really connect with the couple, the female sure, but also the male because they're sort of partners in keeping the female safe."

"Yeah, no pressure. Just a lifetime commitment to make a decision in a few minutes."

Tracy laughed. "It's not always like that. I only knew Gabe for a day though. Sometimes you just know when it's right."

161

Which, Michelle had to admit was true.

Akio took that moment to turn around and see them both staring at him. Well now. He was long and lithe, his dark hair loose, framing a face that would have dried the spit in any thinking woman's mouth in seconds flat.

"Damn," she whispered to Tracy.

"Right?" Tracy waved and he began to make his way over.

Josh moved to them, pausing to kiss Michelle. "Sorry, I got caught up. Rose wanted to show me the picture she drew of Milton."

Akio approached and Josh held a hand out that Akio took. "Akio, this is my mate, Michelle. Michelle, this is Akio Minami. He's part of the Enforcer corps in Boston. He's here with Jack and the wolves from National."

She smiled and he took her hand. "It's nice to meet you. Josh was telling us all about you on the way over from the airport."

He had a great accent. So much Boston in it.

As she chatted with Akio, Josh put an arm around her shoulders and she leaned into him, looking up at him with a smile. He'd seen this dozens of times. A member of his pack when they'd come to a Joining with a new bonded mate. He'd always thought it was great, but now that it was him, he understood the ridiculous smiles, the way they'd needed to touch so much.

As it was, wolves needed that contact. They were a touchy-feely group. But every time he put his hands on her, it soothed him, excited him, made him feel like he'd just won something awesome.

And there was something between Akio and Michelle. Akio was the kind of male who listened more than he talked. Which was a quality Josh respected a great deal. But he came out of his shell when he was around people he genuinely enjoyed.

Like he was doing just then. Charming Michelle with stories of Boston and the wolves there.

Akio paused, a hand on her arm, when Jack called his name. "I'm sorry to interrupt. I need to go see what he needs. I'm sure we'll talk more." Akio smiled and nodded to Josh before he headed to see what Jack needed.

"You're here! And look at you, the bond looks good on you." Gina came over and pulled Michelle into a hug.

"Hi there." Michelle smiled at Gina, and Josh realized she'd already made friends. He was totally grateful for that. They chatted, and Josh scanned the room automatically, always alert for any problems.

Akio stood with Nick and Jack, everyone wearing serious faces. Truth be told, he'd thought Akio would be an excellent choice as an anchor. He was strong and smart. And he lived across the country so while he would of course be at their home for the holidays and that sort of thing, he wouldn't be in their same pack or the same city.

It would be easier on them all that way. He'd seen anchors pining for the woman they could not have, and he didn't wish that on anyone. He wanted Michelle to be close and comfortable with her anchor, but he sure as fuck didn't want any other male being in love with his woman. The distance would help with that.

Damon came over and hugged Michelle, and Josh nearly socked him in the face. He didn't stop a growl, which made Michelle tense up and give him a look laced with apprehension. Funny, he hadn't felt nearly this possessive when Akio had just touched Michelle. Another point to him as a possible anchor.

Gina snorted a laugh and patted Michelle's arm. "They're all like this with mates. Damon too. They don't really mean anything by it. Have you had anything to eat yet?"

"Let's get a toast and introduce Michelle to the pack." Tracy took Gabe's hand as he approached.

"Oh good idea." Josh bent and dropped a kiss on Michelle's cheek. "Welcome, beautiful, to Pacific."

Michele blushed and Josh breathed her in deep.

Tracy bustled off to gather everyone for the official Joining, and Michelle turned to Josh. "So I get on my knees and say what to them?"

"We'll both do it, side by side. All you'll need to do is agree to swear fealty. You're not a wolf, but through me, you share my rank. By swearing fealty, you're agreeing to shepherd the wolves in Pacific, to keep them safe and keep their best interests foremost in your words and deeds."

She nodded and took the glass of champagne Tracy handed her.

Tracy whistled loud and everyone gave her their attention.

"Tonight we give witness to the Joining of Michelle Slattery, mate to Josh Neelan, to Pacific."

There were hoots and applause as Michelle looked over the room. So amazing to be welcomed like this. So many faces, openly friendly, smiling, pleased to welcome her.

Josh put a little pressure on her arm so she knew to kneel with him in front of the Alpha trio. "Michelle, do you swear fealty to Pacific and its wolves?"

"I do."

And then her magick rose, swirled around and seemed to mix with theirs. Knitting, in a sense, her essence to the energy of the pack.

Josh looked over at her with a smile. She felt his pleasure through the link. His happiness and love.

Nick helped her up and turned her to face the group. "Welcome, Michelle, to Pacific and best wishes on your bond to Josh."

More raised glasses and cheers as people came forward to introduce themselves, kiss her cheek or rub their faces along her jaw.

"It's a gesture of affection and respect," Akio murmured, as he appeared at her side, explaining the cheek-rubbing thing.

"Ah, gotcha. Thanks."

He inclined his head.

After what seemed like forever with the cheek rubs and the kisses and welcomes, they headed into a huge dining room where a buffet dinner had been laid out. They filled plates and milled around until Gina approached them.

She pointed to a couch in a far corner where Damon sat. "We saved you guys a place."

They all followed her over and put their drinks down on the nearby coffee table. Josh grinned at Damon. "It's out of the way of traffic but near enough to the food."

Akio was already sitting with them, and Jack came over and sat next to Akio as they all chatted about Enforcer-type stuff. Michelle had expected to feel excluded or bored, but the stuff they talked about was a lot like cop work and she found herself offering suggestions and asking questions.

Feeling like she could belong after all.

She and Gina had escaped outside to stand on the huge back deck watching a large group of kids play with Milton, Tracy's ridiculously sweet and goofy lab. He looked as if he might just pass out with the joy of all the giggles and pets he was getting.

They'd chatted about every day things, about the next get-together with the Owen witches in Portland and how it would now be a welcome dinner for Michelle. Gina helped her understand the current politics within Clan Owen, the clash of old world and the rules which had kept witches safe for the last century or so, and the decidedly more modern views held by Meriel Owen, who wanted to come out to the humans before something bad happened and they were outed anyway.

Michelle tended to agree with Meriel's perspective.

She appreciated all Gina's help and advice, and it was nice to have the beginnings of a new friendship as well. She had a lot to learn. A lot to understand, and people seemed to be going out of their way to help her. It made things better. A little less confusing.

They talked about the threat the mages posed. Gina filled her in on how a group of them had worked with Dominic Bright's mother, who was a turned witch. They'd ambushed Dominic, who was Meriel's husband, and led the Owen Clan at her side, and had tried to kill and drain them. It had been the start of all this madness with missing witches and had been getting increasingly worse.

They had no answers. Michelle had spoken with Lark earlier about finding Allie. They suspected a very bad something was at work, but there were so many unanswered questions and the unsettled nature of it left Michelle uneasy.

Sometimes cases just went unsolved. She knew that. But this was more than a usual case. Others would keep on disappearing until they figured it out. Allie had been a casualty, but there were others who needed to be avenged and she'd do all she could to help that happen.

Josh came out as Gina went in. He kissed Michelle's temple and she leaned into him. "You all right, beautiful?"

Unconditional

"Yes. It's been a lovely evening. I just needed the air and some quiet." It had gotten louder and louder inside until she'd had to escape it out there in the dark.

He laughed quietly. "Wolves can be a raucous bunch. I can't tell you how many people have stopped to tell me how much they enjoyed meeting you tonight. You're making friends right and left."

"Even Esme."

He cringed, and she laughed, poking his side. "She was nice. Apologized for the situation the other day at Tracy's house. It's fine. She knows you're mine, and as long as it stays that way, things are great. I'd hate to have to kill her."

He squeezed her to his side. "It only makes me hot when you talk that way."

"You're weird."

"I am. Listen, so about the anchor thing...I don't want to rush you, but time is getting short. The longer you go without one, the harder it will be for you to manage everything. All the stuff between us, all the emotion traveling through the link is incredibly intense and it can swamp you, make it hard to think and get through. Your anchor will settle down the background noise."

She sighed. It wasn't Josh's fault. He was up front with her. She did this knowing she had to deal with everything that came with the bond, the good and the bad and the plain old weird. "So my choices were the people I met tonight?"

"Yes."

"What do you think?"

"It's more what *you* think. I know each of them would be honored to serve as your anchor, but this is someone you're going to be connected to for the rest of your life. It's your choice to make."

"Well yes, but you'll be connected to them too."

"True. Keeping in mind that the decision is ultimately yours, I think Akio is an excellent choice. He's a good man. A good wolf. Strong and vicious when he has to be. Connected to his pack, he takes his responsibilities seriously. You two clearly like each other."

"I liked all the truffles you introduced me to."

"Truffles?"

"Box of chocolates. Remember?"

He laughed, pulling her close for a kiss and then another for good measure.

"I liked them all, but Akio is the one I clicked with the most. He does what you do. What I do in my own way."

As if they'd called his name, Akio came outside and started a little when he saw them. He eased against a post a few feet away, Josh between them.

"It's funny how normal life can be, even when everything all around is dire and full of sadness." He indicated the kids on the lawn beyond. "I'm sorry for the loss of your friend."

"Thank you."

To have lost so much in the same week she gained everything seemed a cruel joke. Or maybe it was balance. She didn't know. But that didn't matter. Because it was what it was, and she had choices to make and things to do.

She supposed it was what happened to you when you grew up pretty much on your own. You could give up and let things happen to you, weep and moan about the unfairness of it all. Or you could deal with what you've got and make the most of every moment.

Allie had been a bright light in Michelle's life. And it was snuffed out and that hurt beyond bearing. At the same time, Allie would have been the first to high five Michelle over Josh.

She'd been a remarkable person, and she would have whapped Michelle in the back of her head and told her to get on with stuff that needed doing.

And for absolute sure that meant finding the monsters who'd killed Allie and making them pay for it. That would happen if it took the rest of her days.

But for the immediate future, she needed to do this tri-bond deal. And she had a life here in Portland now. So much to learn about herself and her gifts too. So much it was dizzying, and yet, it was a gift to have this man, this community. Allie would have liked this. After she forgave Josh of course. But she'd have been thrilled, and that made it just a little bit better.

She leaned into Josh and blew out a breath, nearly purring when he stroked his knuckles down the back of her neck.

For a while they all stood in the evening cool. The air around them clean and crisp. The sound of the kids was soothing, as was the company. Neither male spoke simply to fill up space. She liked that a great deal.

Finally Akio shifted and took a deep breath. "I wanted to say, away from everyone else, but with both of you present, that I'd be very honored to serve as your anchor." Akio turned his body to them, gaze solemn.

Josh looked to her, letting her choose.

"We were just discussing this. I don't know, is there some sort of official way to do this?" She lifted her hands, hopelessly out of her element.

Akio stepped closer and held his hand out. Josh took one and then held his free hand out to her. She took it.

"It's all what we make of it. Would you like to come over to our apartment?"

Akio nodded.

Chapter Twelve

"Are you nervous?" Josh asked as they waited for Akio to approach after he'd parked his car.

She opened her mouth to agree, but...

Instead, he smiled, slow and sexy. "No. You're hot for it. And that's all right. Can I tell you it's making me hot too?"

"I should be ashamed."

He laughed, spinning to press her into the wall. He rolled his hips, his cock hard, a brand at her belly.

"Yeah? Why? Why be ashamed? Hm? I'm here. I'm yours. You're mine. There's no dispute of that is there?"

She shook her head, catching her bottom lip between her teeth.

"You want this. It makes me hot all over that you do. You're beautiful and sexy and utterly desirable. That you're all mine and for this brief moment we can share with this one other person makes me..." He breathed in deep at her neck. "Fills me with a bottomless, aching need. I want to watch you with him. He's up for it."

They both turned their attention to Akio who'd reached them.

"Aren't you?"

That's when she realized he would have heard the entire exchange.

One corner of his mouth tipped up, and her breath caught at the feral beauty of his features. "Yes. Very much so. From the first moment I saw your magick floating around you like fairy dust."

"Let's go inside before the neighbors call the cops." She laughed, but the sound was breathy and laden with sex.

In the elevator both men crowded against her, and she had to close her eyes at the wave of sensuality that swallowed her.

They all got into Josh's place. Or their place. Whatever, they all got inside, and she was against a wall again, both men pressing against her.

"I'm going to kiss you," Akio said, his voice a low rumble.

"Yes." She tipped her head back, and he lowered his mouth to hers, slowly, so achingly slow at first, giving her a chance to escape.

Josh's hands rested at her hips, tightening as Akio's lips finally touched hers. His taste slid into her system, spicing Josh's. Heightening the moment as his tongue danced along hers.

He might have been a quiet, thoughtful male at the pack house, but this male was nothing if not in total charge of his sexuality.

Josh began to kiss up the side of her neck as her skin sensitized to the point of near pain. Each brush of lips, the scratch of his beard nearly made her sob into Akio's kiss.

Josh's hands slid up her sides, slowly unbuttoning the bodice of her dress, and while she still gasped from the way he'd just pinched her nipple through her bra, his attention shifted to Akio, who turned and tangled tongues with him. The kiss of two became a kiss of three, the focus shifted from two to three, and she groaned at how hot it was.

"If you don't take this off now, it's going to get ripped." Josh turned to her, putting her hands on her belly where the last buttons were still done up.

"Bedroom."

"If you'd allow me?" Akio gestured and she nodded. He bent and picked her up. She wrapped her legs around his waist as his hands held her ass.

She tipped back enough to get her dress unbuttoned by the time he set her on the edge of the bed and stepped away to take her in.

His wolf shone in his gaze and she approved. Josh's eyes went green when his wolf surfaced, but Akio's went amber, and as the two of them stood next to each other, looking at her like she was a rabbit they had just cornered, they stole her breath.

This anchor thing was pretty damned sweet so far.

Akio went to his knees in front of her, moving her hands and drawing the dress from her shoulders. Josh got to the bed behind her, his mouth cruising over her shoulder and neck as his hands pushed her bra down to free her breasts.

"So beautiful, Michelle." Akio said this as Josh pulled the dress from her upper body and then let it fall down. She had to lift, and Akio drew it the rest of the way off, taking her underwear with it.

He traced the marks Josh had left on the sides of her breasts. "This makes my cock hard."

"She's so tasty I have to take a bite here and there."

She shivered and both men moaned softly. Josh's fingers rolled and tugged her nipples while Akio kissed her knee, his fingers running up the inside of her thigh, brushing against her pussy and away again.

"I can scent you," Josh whispered, his mouth against her ear, making her shiver again. "Do you want his mouth on you?"

"Y-esss," she answered, unable to deny it.

Akio's eyes locked on hers as he drew his tongue up her thigh before he spread her legs wide.

"I'm going to need my hands, Josh. Hold her open for me."

Josh shifted to grab her thighs and keep them wide.

His position effectively kept her upper body trapped, so she sank her fingers into the bedding as Akio used his thumbs to part her labia and take a long lick.

She moaned low in her throat and Josh echoed the sound. So much need emanated from her skin, he licked up her neck, tasting it.

Akio bent over her cunt, licking, sucking, fucking her with his tongue, his hair sliding over Josh's hands as he held Michelle open wide.

Oh, yes there was sexual chemistry between the three of them, no doubt. Akio would have been Josh's choice as well. The way he moved, touched Michelle only made him hotter. He already believed Michelle to be the sexiest female alive, that another male thought so too worked in ways he wasn't sure he could really explain.

So he went with it.

"What do you like? Hm?" Akio's hoarse whisper brought a strangled moan from Michelle's lips.

"You're doing just fine," she mumbled.

Akio backed up, his mouth not quite touching her pussy. "Oh, no. You see, I can only have you this once. I mean to make it the best it can be."

Her laugh was frustrated and amused at the same time. "Goddamn shifter males! Get to work."

That made all three of them laugh.

"She likes it when you suck on her clit." Josh's gaze locked with Akio's, and he watched as Akio lowered his mouth and did what Josh had suggested.

She arched on a cry but Josh held her in place as she writhed.

"Ah, you were right about that." Akio grinned and then fluttered the flat of his tongue against her, wrenching a ragged moan from her this time. "That seems to do the trick as well."

"You two are going to kill me," she snarled, trying to get nearer to Akio's mouth when he'd pulled back to speak.

"No we aren't, beautiful. We're going to make you come. A lot."

Akio bent over her cunt again, alternating between licking and sucking her clit until she inhaled a huge breath and then blew it out on a gut-deep moan. The muscles of her thighs tightened as she strained against his hold and came hard and fast.

Still clothed, Akio lunged up and took her mouth, kissing her, his hair screening them from view.

"You taste like magick and sex," he said against her mouth as he pulled back.

"You taste like me," she replied, and both men groaned. Josh let go of her legs, and she leaned back against him, looking up into his face. "You're not naked. Also, so...is this anchor thing between the three of us in every way?"

Akio still lay across her, kissing over her collarbone, hands skimming over her body. He looked up, pausing to kiss her chin. "It doesn't have to be. There's one necessary part, that's me, sliding my cock into your pussy until I come."

She grinned down at Akio and up at Josh, who bent to kiss her.

"What do you want it to be?"

She slid her hand up to cup the back of his neck. "This is all pretty intense, but clearly there's something between you two." She shrugged. "Not like I'm going to complain if the two of you are together too."

"Why don't we just do whatever feels okay as we go?" Since the bond, she'd become central to him, she'd already been part of him for as long as he could remember, but now making her happy, loving her, protecting her, had become part of that. Was it hot to kiss Akio a few minutes earlier? Yes. But he didn't want the focus to shift or to make her feel anything but good.

And as hot as Akio was, as hot as it was to watch him lick over Michelle's nipples right then, she was on loan. For a limited time. Josh just wanted to be extra sure that everyone knew what was up so that no one got hurt.

"All right. You're still not naked though." Her gaze was only for him right then, and he was helpless to do anything but kiss her long and slow until she'd gone all warm and boneless against him.

Josh finally broke away, and she shifted, rolling to shove his shirt from his body, licking over his nipples until they'd hardened enough to scrape her teeth over the way she knew he liked.

She got his pants open and shoved down, and he moved from the bed to get them off. She turned to Akio. "You're not naked either."

"As you wish." He crossed his hands over and grabbed the hem of his shirt, pulling it from his body, revealing a great deal of beautiful ink.

She got to her knees and moved closer. "Wow, this is amazing."

"A lot of wolves can't keep the ink after a shift. Tracy has her ink, I know some others. This is fantastic." Josh spoke from behind Akio.

She moved his hair aside and studied the intricate lines making up birds in flight. On his back an incredibly detailed pair of wings that took up pretty much all his skin.

"Incredible."

He turned, a wicked grin on his mouth. "I haven't even opened my pants yet."

She laughed, appreciating his sense of humor and the way it kept things light and fun even though it was also intense.

"Well, go on then. We're waiting. Wow me, Akio."

She leaned back into Josh, who slid his hands up her arms and up her neck, holding her that way, lightly collared.

"She likes that." Akio stepped from his shoes and unbuttoned and unzipped his pants, sliding them off along with his shorts. His cock sprang free, and she swallowed back the *wow* that she nearly said. She didn't want to make anyone feel bad and two men in her space, two really well-endowed men and she was mated to one and his equipment was mighty fine but she knew dudes could be touchy about that stuff.

Still. "Yeah, that's incredible too." She licked her lips.

"I think you should get to your knees and suck his cock." Josh whispered this, his breath against the skin of her ear, rendering her weak in the knees.

"You should join him." She guided him to stand next to Akio before she went to her knees.

It wasn't like she had threesomes every day so she was naturally comfortable with it. Or had them ever. But something had come over her and she embraced it. She felt so much for Josh, and a true connection with Akio, who was entering their relationship in his own way. Taking on responsibility for her in such an elemental way.

It made her feel sexy and special and important, and that enabled her to leave all her awkwardness behind and let go. Enjoy this moment for what it was.

She ran her cheek across the line of Akio's cock and then did the same with Josh. They both felt different, had a different scent. Something rose inside her, reaching through her connection to Josh and pulled them closer. He reached out and took her shoulder with a grunt.

Amazing.

She licked over the head of Akio's cock and then Josh's. Mirroring each movement. Each lick. She rimmed the crown of each cock, held a sac in each palm before she slid her hands up and moved them both at the hip to face each other. She grabbed their cocks at the root and held them together.

"Yes." She spoke really to herself, but both men groaned, which made her feel like a sex goddess.

Josh watched down his body to where his woman knelt, his cock in her fist along with Akio's. Nearly lost it when she licked over the heads and he felt the corresponding throb and gasp of Akio. Each one of them looked down, wonder on their faces.

He thrust into her fist, sliding along Akio's cock. Akio looked up at him, one brow rising slowly as he thrust in answer.

Michelle hummed her delight. This side of her was unexpected. Nearly hedonistic and he dug it.

He leaned in and grabbed Akio's hair around his fist and pulled him closer for a kiss.

Kissing a man was different than kissing a woman. Kissing the anchor was a whole different thing entirely. Kissing anyone but Michelle after they'd bonded? He felt her in the back of his consciousness, like spice to this moment. Akio tasted like her, like Josh's mate.

He growled, possessive, greedy for more, greedy of her very essence.

Akio growled back as the kiss deepened, a gnash of teeth and tongue. As Michelle took the heads of their cocks into her mouth in a tight, hard suck, his fingertips dug into her shoulder and yanked Akio's hair harder.

She kissed down both cocks, drawing her tongue over the root of each, down over their balls and up again. It was so good he found himself making little deals with himself as to when he'd stop. Little equations as to how close he could get without coming.

Because he wanted to save that for her. Inside her after Akio had finished. His wolf knew that had to be the way of it. Yes, this other male could mark her this once. But he would come after, fill his mate with *his* seed.

"Too close, little witch." Akio gasped as he placed a gentle hand on her head, a caress followed. "I need to save that for when I'm inside you." He stepped back with a slow breath, and Josh helped her up, pulling her close.

"Your lips are all swollen."

Her eyes had that blur she got when she was really turned on. His wolf was very close to the surface, driven by Akio, who was in a similar state. This female, his mate, dripping with magick and sex, held endless fascination for wolf and man.

"I'm going to fuck you now." Akio stood just behind her, sandwiching her between them.

"Right-O."

Her voice was breathy, and she leaned her head back on Akio's shoulder.

Josh's hands slid up her belly to her breasts, always back to those it seemed, and her hips jutted forward when he tugged on her nipples.

"I love that," he murmured.

"That works out because I do too." Her smile was only for him.

Akio walked her to the bed and rolled onto his back. She stood at the edge and looked at him, Josh at her side.

"All that hair is so beautiful," she said quietly. Where Josh was big and braw, muscular, tawny skinned and outdoorsy, Akio was lithe and powerful. Tall. Absolutely powerfully built, but more like a swimmer or a cyclist. He was utterly beautiful and she was going to have sex with him and it was totally all right with her boyfriend. Mate. Yes, him.

She climbed over his body, straddling his waist, her fingers digging into all that hair spread out all around him.

"Ride me," Akio said, his voice raspy.

Josh got behind her, pressed to her back. "Lift up." She did, and he angled Akio's cock, stroking the head against her until she slid slowly down, taking him inside her body.

With Josh behind her this way, it was like he was part of it. Her link to him was so strong she knew he felt what she did, knew that while she enjoyed this moment with Akio, it was Josh who filled her thoughts of forever.

Akio's hands slid up her thighs and met Josh's at her hips. They joined fingers and both grasped her there. She closed her eyes and leaned back as Josh took her weight.

She lost track of time as both men caressed her skin until Akio growled and shook her from that place she'd drifted off to.

"Josh, make her come."

Well, that certainly got her attention!

One of Josh's hands caressed down her belly to her clit while the other held her breast out for Akio to roll and tug a nipple.

So much. Too much. She closed her eyes to try to find some control but couldn't resist opening them again to look down at the man below her, at two sets of hands on her body, to be enticed and seduced by the scent of the room. Magick rose from her in reaction, so sharp it nearly hurt.

Josh's mouth cruised to the spot where her neck met her body. His teeth grazed her there once, twice, and then he struck, his teeth digging into the flesh, into the muscle, and she came. So hard all the breath left her in one exhale of sound.

Akio cursed, sped beneath her, thrusting up to meet her body as she came down. The fingers on her nipple tightened, and he snarled, coming.

The anchor bond slammed into her and she lost her equilibrium again. Dimly she was aware of Josh picking her up off Akio, pulling her into his arms, his mouth brushing her cheeks, speaking soft endearments as this new bond found a way to work with the one already in place.

Akio kissed her forehead, and she knew he left the bed as the magick of the bond drew her away from that movement and deep into herself.

Josh looked up from where she snuggled into his body. Akio was getting dressed. "Thank you." Not just for that moment, but for the commitment he'd just made to Michelle.

Akio nodded. "It was my pleasure. Thank you for sharing your bond with me."

"You're welcome to stay over. Especially since we're going over to the crime scene tomorrow morning."

"I think you two need the time alone so I'm going to head out." Akio reached out to take one of Michelle's hands, kissing it. "I'll see you tomorrow, little witch."

She dragged her eyelids up, a smile on her lips. "Okay. Thank you, Akio." She blushed and both men chuckled. "I mean, yeah, thanks."

"I told Josh already, but I promise you it was my pleasure."

"Come over early and I'll make a big breakfast."

Akio nodded and was gone. Josh turned his attention to her once more. "Hey, beautiful, you all right?"

"It's sort of a mini-version of the bond with you. I'm feeling better now."

"Yeah? How much better?" He needed her. Not if it would hurt her or bring her discomfort. But his wolf was anxious to stamp over Akio's presence.

Her gaze sharpened, and she managed to sit up and straddle him. "Why is that, Josh? Hm?"

He slowly got her to her back, looming over her. "I..."

"Need to be in me because another male just was?"

"Sounds petty."

She shook her head. "No it doesn't. Come on in."

And as he slid into her body, he came home.

Chapter Thirteen

She got up and took a shower, saving her tears for when she had time behind a closed door. She'd woken up after a dream where she'd been back at the house they'd found Allie.

The memory of her friend's broken body echoed through her like she'd been punched in the gut.

Of course Josh sensed her upset through the link and barged in.

"What's wrong?" He pulled the enclosure door open.

"I'm living with a man who doesn't knock on a closed bathroom door?"

He simply got in the enclosure with her, crowding her, pulling her close. "Living with a wolf. Comes with the territory."

"I just had a dream about Allie."

He took over, washing her hair as she stood there, sort of stunned by this big, powerful male tending to her so gently. He was so...tender with her. It made her tears come again.

"I'm sorry. I don't normally cry this much," she muttered.

"If anyone got to cry, you get to this week. There's no shame in mourning someone you lost. I'm sorry. I wish I could make it better. I wish the end of the story was different."

"You are making it better. Without you I probably wouldn't even have found her, and even if I had, I'd be alone. This thing between us, this bond? It makes everything better."

He tipped her chin up as he soaped her body. "Thank you for that. You're okay about...everything this morning?"

She couldn't help it, she laughed. "After my three-way you mean?" He tried to appear stern but failed. "Yes, I'm fine. I mean, it might be awkward when he comes over for pancakes, but it felt...right, when we were doing it."

"It was beautiful. You're beautiful, and I ache that you're having to go through this pain."

"I'm alive. I'm in love and have so much ahead of me. Allie doesn't have any of that. If it's the last thing I do, I will find the people who did this to her. Who destroyed her future."

"I'll be with you the whole way."

They got out and she made a big breakfast, as promised. Though cooking for werewolves was a challenge because she had to make so much more than she normally would.

Right on time, there was a tap on the door and Josh let Akio in.

He moved to her and she realized there was a link to him too. Not as all-encompassing as the one she shared with Josh, but she could feel his pleasure at seeing her. Affection. It was nice to have someone see her and feel so happy.

He kissed her cheek and handed her a huge bouquet of flowers.

She put them in water as he and Josh got coffee and put out plates before they all sat at the table to eat before they headed out. Their connection was easy, and she began to understand what Gina had meant when she'd talked about their connection with her anchor.

Akio was dear to her. He was part of her now and she part of him. She didn't need to be a wolf to understand it. It just was and it pleased her to hear him speak. The rumble of his accent as it accented Josh's.

And where Josh was snarly when other males had been affectionate to her, he seemed fine with the way Akio would touch her from time to time. How he'd stolen food from her plate and she'd laughed.

Even when he'd hugged her when she'd nearly cried as she'd described the situation at the crime scene. Josh had handed her a box of tissues, and both males had watched her carefully, features full of concern.

"Are you sure you want to do this?" Akio asked from the back seat as they pulled away from the apartment and headed to the scene. "You can stay back here. Josh can take me. I need the scents, I can get it without you. Neither of us wants you unnecessarily upset."

"He's right." Josh worried about her too. "I don't want you hurting any more than you have to."

"Look, yes, this is my friend, but I'm a cop. It's what I do. And frankly at least this way I can feel like I'm doing *something* to find whoever is responsible. It's not my ideal way to spend a Sunday morning, but it needs to be done."

Akio squeezed her shoulder, and Josh let his concern and comfort flow through the link. He knew it was hard sometimes for newly bonded pairs to share through the link, but maybe it was due to having known her so long, things seemed to be all right on that front.

She was open with him, affectionate, accepting of the bond and fairly laid-back when it came to how dominant he could get. So far anyway.

Akio kept her occupied as they drove, asking her questions about her former job and what she planned for her future. He skirted asking if she'd consider the change. Many human mates made the choice to take on a wolf. But heaven knew she had enough on her plate just then. It was something he could bring up later on but for the time being, they had other things to work through.

"It's just up here. Don't take the driveway. I want to walk it again." Michelle had pulled into herself. Her eyes had shifted from the warmth of his mate to cold, flat cop eyes.

"I'm going to shift," Akio said as they pulled off to the side of the road. "I can scent better this way."

"Good idea. I'll get your clothes in my pack so you can shift back up at the house if you want or need to."

Two minutes later Akio handed Josh his rolled-up jeans and shirt, along with his shoes.

The flat cop eyes were gone as Michelle scrambled to turn and look. "Can I watch? You shift I mean." She blushed.

Akio brushed his fingertips over her cheek. "You can have whatever you like, little witch." He winked and she laughed. Josh was grateful for that moment of levity. The heaviness of her heart was palpable through the link. He ached to make something better that no one and nothing could.

A wash of magick rushed through the car as Akio shifted, pulling at Josh's wolf. A lower-ranked shifter might have succumbed to that siren song, but Josh just breathed in deep and rode it out until he could see clearly again.

"Beautiful." She reached out to touch Akio's fur. His wolf was obsidian with a splash of honey-gold on his chest.

Akio's wolf head butted her and shook himself out, and she opened his door to let him out.

Michelle put her cop back on and they headed up to the house. She tried to compartmentalize it. The job had taught her how to put all her personal feelings to the side when she was working. To view a crime scene in a certain way, and she worked really hard to do just that.

Akio had stalked off, sniffing and doing his wolf business. Josh was beside her, his gaze shifting, taking in every detail as they moved.

"They would have brought her up here in a car. She was close to dead by that point if the time of death they called was right."

They'd gone through the house rather thoroughly but she did it again. It wasn't a big space, but the stench of death magic seemed to have sunk into the walls and floors.

"I'm not even a witch and I can sense all the bad stuff in the air." Josh kept close, though not in the way should she need to draw her weapon.

"Whatever they did here killed so much of the natural energies all around." It was unnaturally silent, the air hung too heavy. "I don't see any of her energy in the house at all. Just some on the back porch." They walked out the back door and she indicated a corner.

Akio came around the corner and sneezed a few times, shaking his head.

Josh spoke, "Yeah, I know. It's all wrong here."

Though she didn't want to with all her heart, she needed to get back to that circle where they'd had Allie.

Haltingly at first, she headed that way. Akio brushed against her legs and Josh put an arm around her shoulders. "We're here with you. Just take it as slowly as you need to."

She squeezed his hand and ran her other along Akio's fur, drawing strength as she took the scene in through her othersight.

Dark, ugly smudges of energy. The stolen magic used to fuel whatever they'd done to Allie was gone, but the aftereffects of it were still smeared over the area like an ugly film.

She shielded herself the best she could. "You two wait outside the circle."

Akio snorted and Josh simply ignored her.

"Look." She turned to face Josh. "I don't know if I can protect either of you if something goes wrong. There's some fucked-up magic here, stuff way beyond my skill level. You can sniff from out there or we're leaving."

Josh touched her cheek. "I don't like you not within reach."

"I don't like that my best friend was murdered. So you know, lots of stuff happens that we don't like." She sent a look to Akio who stood at Josh's side. "You too. Outside the circle or I'm out of here."

"If anything looks remotely hinky, I'm coming in there and grabbing you." Josh crossed his arms over his chest which, in addition to making him look stern, also bulged up his muscles. Damn he looked good.

One of his brows slid up which meant he knew what she was thinking. She rolled her eyes and turned around, getting to her knees in the circle, her hands hovering just above the earth there.

Akio circled where she knelt, his nose to the ground, and Josh prowled around, never getting too very far from her.

She used a spell Lark had described to her over the phone to try to discern how many different mages had been there. She could pick up two mages, along with Allie, and there was something else.

She paused, brushing her fingertips over a patch of ground, and it was like she'd opened a drawer or pulled the lid off something. The power of it, whatever it was, flooded her, crashing past the shields she'd erected to defend herself.

Dark.

Horrible. So horrible and overflowing with bad things, there was nothing else, only cold and loneliness. It filled her veins with lead even as all she wanted to do was move away as fast as she could.

Her senses all seemed to be jumbled up, fighting against each other as she froze, trying to run but not having the will to do it.

He was fine watching her until she brushed her fingertips over a spot in the dirt and then something *wrong* spilled through the area. It made him want to slip his skin and snarl. Wanted to run away as fast as he could.

He might have simply done that if it hadn't been for her. It rolled over her, and their link, which until that moment had been fully open between them, had gone from warm and vibrant to a rush of ice. The fullness of their exchange narrowed, choking, dwindling the amount of sensory exchange to nearly nothing.

Akio growled low, stalking between Josh and where Michelle crouched inside the circle.

He looked back over his shoulder at Josh and then growled louder, leaping at Josh, shoving him back and freeing him from whatever feedback loop he'd been caught in.

"Thanks," he called as he stepped back to her, grabbing her body below her arms and yanking her free. The energy of his motion knocked them both flying back and onto the dirt with a bone-jarring thud.

She was limp in his arms and he shook her slightly. "What? What? Michelle, speak to me right now." Fear rushed through his veins. Aside from the pack, nothing and no one had been important to him the way she was. That anything threatened her well-being made him no little unstable.

So pale. Damn it. He took her cheeks in his hands, touched his forehead to hers and rushed through their bond, yanking her back from wherever or whatever had tried to take her from him.

He found it, the golden thread that bound them together, and he yanked it as hard as he could with a mental snarl, pulling her close.

A flush rose to her neck and cheeks as she gasped a deep breath and then gagged violently.

She turned to her side and threw up as she feebly tried to push Josh's hands away but he had no interest in letting her go. He held her hair from her face and rubbed a hand up and down her back.

Akio had shifted back and pulled on a pair of pants. He knelt next to them, a hand on Josh's knee as they watched her finally get herself under control.

She shook so hard he stood and picked her up. She didn't argue at all, which concerned him enough to start heading to the car. Akio followed, pulling a shirt on but foregoing shoes.

He nearly ran to the car, trying not to jostle her too much.

Akio reached around them and opened the door so Josh could put her in the front seat gently.

"I'm taking you to the hospital." He knew he probably stunk of fear, but he didn't care. She needed help.

She shook her head and then winced. "No, I'm all right. They can't help with what's wrong anyway."

"Fuck that, Michelle. You're not in my shoes. We'll go to Gina's then. *Someone* needs to look at you."

"I understand you're worried. But no one can help me. I'm all right. Or I will be in a while."

Akio leaned forward, his hands moved to her shoulders. "What happened, little witch? You gave us a scare. You need to cut us a break."

She reached up and squeezed his hands while she looked to Josh. She was still pale, and the stench of his fear and that wrong energy hung in the car heavily, rendering his wolf skittish and unsettled.

"There is something...else. Not a mage. Not a turned witch. Something I've never felt before. More than that, they took shifters too. They smelled like Pacific wolves," she mumbled as he pulled away from the curb.

They had a few MIA wolves, but that hadn't been public knowledge. In fact he'd been inclined to believe the wolves they hadn't heard from were just temporarily out of pocket. Some traveled for business, some could have been on a vacation.

"I didn't smell any other wolves there." Akio spoke quietly as he kept his hands on her shoulders.

She gulped water from the bottle Josh handed her.

"No, not on the ground. In the magic. In...whatever it was I felt. It took power from all sorts of Others. Not just witches. Whatever it is, it's bad. So so bad."

Akio made a low, frustrated sound. "We knew they were taking wolves. But this... Listen, we need to go to Boston, Josh. Right now. I need her to talk to Cade about this whole thing. The wolves need to know what is happening."

The imperative to protect his people drove Josh. Filled his veins until he couldn't think straight.

She reached out and squeezed his hand. "I feel it too. I guess it happened when we joined or whatever. I know you need to talk to Cade. I can call Clan Owen from the airport or whatever."

"At least let Gina meet us at the airport before we go. You were out! I had to use the link to get you."

"And you did. I'm here. I'm working on being fine again. Gina's not a doctor or a nurse. I'm the one who felt it. I'll describe it to someone at Owen. I promise."

He frowned.

"I'd kiss you to reassure you, but I have vomit breath. Which is not romantical in the least."

"I'll arrange a flight out as soon as possible." Akio leaned close enough to kiss the top of Michelle's head. "You scared the hell out of me. Let's not do that again, all right?"

She saluted him and leaned back into the seat, closing her eyes as he plotted the ways he'd kill whoever had done this to his mate.

Akio spoke low on his phone, making arrangements to get back to Boston. Internally, he was relieved to be taking her there instead of Seattle. Witch politics were outside his scope, but he understood wolf politics and he could protect her better with that knowledge. He knew the witches had their own response to this kidnapping thing, but it involved more than just them. Wolves were being taken now. And he'd do whatever he had to to protect his people.

"I need you to talk to Tracy, Nick and Gabe too."

She sighed. "I *need* to brush my teeth. And I *need* a shower. At *your* place, not theirs."

He stifled a smile. If she felt well enough to say that, she was getting better. "All right, I'll make you a deal."

"I'm not interested in a deal, Josh. I want to go take a shower and brush my teeth. Where I have my clothes and toothbrush. Then you can haul me to your Alphas and to Boston. But I'm not deal-making for anything else."

Akio snorted but wisely continued his call.

"All right." Josh concentrated on driving and keeping the smile off his face. "Mighty wolfish of you."

She kept her eyes closed. "What is?"

"You want your own territory. It's where you feel safest."

"I don't want to be naked where another female wolf's magick is. Sue me."

He grinned. "Beautiful, it makes me hot when you're like this. It appeals to my wolf." He took her hand and squeezed it.

She snorted. "Everything appeals to your wolf. He's pretty easy."

Akio laughed then. "She's got your number."

"Only for you. Fine. I'll take you home. To *our* place and you can clean up. I'll call to see if they want to come over or if we can go on our way to the airport." Wasn't like it was an option to keep Cade Warden waiting on such key info. Nick, Tracy and Gabe would know that too.

Chapter Fourteen

After her shower and a great deal of scrubbing the stench of the death magic off her skin, she'd put her hair in a quick ponytail. When she stepped out of the bathroom, Tracy and Gabe were at the apartment, waiting for her.

"I know it's hard, but anything you can tell us about what you felt would really be helpful." Gabe watched her intently as Josh put a mug into her hands.

"Drink that. I made a call to Gage while you were in the shower, and he said tea would help you feel better. He wants you to call and fill him or Lark in on what you felt when you get the chance. They're going to try to send someone down, or at least have a more trained witch go to the scene. But there's something major going on, and they've got all their powerful folks working on figuring out who this big bad is and how to stop it. They don't want just anyone going out there, especially given how you reacted to it." Josh pushed a sandwich her way. "He also said protein helps after you get a shock to your magick the way you did."

Akio sat on her other side, squeezing her shoulder. "Your color is a little better. You will sleep on the trip out to Boston."

Suddenly all that alpha male in the room drowned her. All that attention and concern stifled her, even as she found it reassuring.

Tracy rolled her eyes with a grin and then shrugged. "I know. I grew up in a house full of them and now I have two of my own. You'll get used to it."

"This is nice. I mean, thank you, Josh for the sandwich and for touching base with Owen for me. And thank you, Akio, for your concern. But all this alpha-male smothering is a lot and I need to breathe."

Akio eased back. Only a little. But enough. Gabe smiled and winked at Tracy, who leaned into his body and took up some of his attention.

On the other hand, Josh stared right back at her. "Tough. You scared the hell out of me, Michelle. It's going to take me a while before I can manage to feel any better about it. I need to know you're okay. My wolf needs to take care of you." He tipped his chin. "Eat while you talk."

She sighed but obeyed, eating automatically, and yes, after several bites of the rare roast beef on the sandwich, she did indeed feel better.

In between bites, she explained to Tracy and Gabe what she'd felt at the scene, in the circle, and tried to make sense of the way she'd sensed the energy of Pacific wolves. She was certain they'd stolen the magick from the wolves, the way they had with the witches. But who they were and where they'd gone was still a mystery. And this *new* and altogether terrifying presence she'd picked up at the murder scene made her very concerned.

They didn't overstay their welcome after that. Only urging Josh, Michelle and Akio to stay safe and check in frequently. Michelle needed to pack a quick bag, and they were on the way to the airport where Akio had arranged for a plane to Boston. They'd added Pacific wolves to Jack's team so Akio would be free to fly back to Boston with Josh and Michelle.

"I'll be all right, you know," Michelle murmured to Josh after Akio had gone off to check in and connect with their pilot. "Your job is here. Your job is protecting the Alpha trio and you can't do that if you're with me."

194

"My job is protecting my pack. Which I'm doing by going to Boston. And now my job is protecting my mate. You're out of your fucking mind if you think I'd let you fly across the country without me. Even with Akio. We just mated. You've had an extraordinarily shitty week. I'm with you and that's all there is to it, so don't waste your energy arguing any further."

She leaned against him, sensing how agitated he was, wanting to comfort and soothe. "Okay then." Since they needed to wait until they got all the stuff in place to take off, she took that time to call Owen and ended up with voicemail. She left as detailed a message as she could about what she'd encountered at the scene. About that other sort of magick she'd sensed. Not related to the mages or the turned witches. Something she'd never encountered the likes of before. Even talking about it hours later, it filled her with dread. A dread Josh must have felt through the bond because he pulled her closer, wrapping his arms around her until she felt a little better. It worked both ways.

Akio returned and hustled them onto the plane where she strapped in. The melatonin she'd taken just an hour before began to make her eyelids droop, and it wasn't very long until she gave in and let herself sleep.

Josh kept an arm around her as they flew. Reassured by the slow, deep rise and fall of her chest. Gage had told him once she slept, her magick would begin to heal her and replenish from the shock of what she'd experienced at the murder scene.

Their bond, golden, brilliant and strong, hummed between them, and his wolf eased back. A little. He'd been in a high state of agitation since he'd seen her slump over and their bond had gone pale and thin.

"She's going to be all right." Akio handed him a cup of coffee. "So strong, this one. Witches have a spine of steel. She'll

195

get along well with Renee and Kendra, the witches I know in Boston."

"Renee is Jack's mate and Kendra is her sister, right?"

Akio nodded. "Kendra is mated to Max de La Vega, who is the Alpha of the jaguar jamboree in Boston. She took on a jaguar without being bitten. Her magick just sort of...absorbed it. Insane how powerful these two sisters are. I'd wondered if they were an anomaly. Neither of them operated within a clan or a coven. But I've met other witches since, and the women most especially seem to have the hearts of lions."

Josh snorted. "Too bad they don't have the physical strength of one. She's so fragile. It fills me with terror. You only saw pictures of the results of what they did to Allie. My wolf is not happy at all. Keeps sending me mental images of that as he snarls."

"Not like you're going to be able to manage her." Akio grinned before it faded. "We'll keep her safe. You have my word that I will do all I can. Do you think she'd ever consider taking on the change?"

Some mates who weren't wolves opted to be bitten and go through the change after they were claimed. It made them physically stronger and longer-lived as well. She'd already have a longer life as she was a witch, but the physical strength was something he really liked the idea of.

"I might suggest it. In the future. She's had enough to deal with lately."

Akio nodded. "Would you two consider staying in my home while you're in Boston? It's safer than any hotel. I'm near the pack house and so I can easily up the number of guards. And I'll feel better, safer, if she's safer." He paused. "I know this is hard for you. She's yours. I don't dispute that. But she's mine too in many ways. I just want to protect her."

Josh understood it, though he couldn't have before Akio became their anchor. This male wouldn't ever get between Josh and Michelle. But he loved Michelle because of their bond and would die to protect her. That meant a lot. And he didn't feel threatened. Not like he did when other males came around. His wolf recognized Akio as *theirs* in some sense.

Josh nodded. "I'd appreciate that."

She woke up to Josh kissing her softly. "Hello, beautiful. We'll be landing in a few minutes."

She stretched, feeling a lot better after sleeping pretty much the entire flight. "I'm sorry, did I drool on you?"

He laughed. "Not that I noticed. You didn't even stir as Akio and I talked. You were out. How do you feel?"

"I'm glad I slept. I do feel like my magick has recharged. I'm not feeling dirty the way I did before. Or weighted down by whatever I brushed up against."

"Good."

She stood. "I could totally get used to private-plane travel."

Akio approached, smiling when he caught sight of her awake. "I was just checking with the pilot. You look better." He hugged her before setting her back to look her over carefully.

"I'm fine. Though I will clean up a little before we land."

"Bathroom is through there." Akio pointed.

She grabbed her purse and headed back. Nicely, it wasn't one of those teeny bathrooms they had on commercial flights. This one was roomy, and in the medicine cabinet, it had toothbrushes and other things she'd need to freshen up with.

She brushed her teeth and washed her face, moisturized and dealt with her hair. She was going to meet the king, or supreme Alpha or whatever he was called officially, and that was important to both Josh and Akio so she didn't want to look like she just fell out of bed.

Thank goodness she'd tossed her makeup bag into her purse before she'd left so she could do some basic foundation, blush and some lipstick. By the time she joined Akio and Josh as they'd announced their descent and to get strapped in, she felt a lot more human.

Josh smiled as she took his hand.

"Are you nervous about flying?"

"No." And she realized he must have felt it through the bond. "No, I'm just...I want to make a good impression on Cade and the rest of the wolves. It's sort of like meeting the family, I guess."

"Beautiful, they're going to love you. And they're your family now too. Nothing to be nervous about because you're wonderful. You're going to like Cade and Grace a lot. I promise."

It seemed a lot to promise but she let it go. She wasn't a wolf, after all. But she did love Josh and she hoped they could see it.

Akio leaned out to squeeze her knee. "They're going to love you. Josh radiates joy. You're the reason. If for nothing else, they'd love that. But as it happens, though I'm obviously biased, you're pretty amazing. And courageous. They're going to appreciate your coming all the way across the country to talk to Cade and Grace in person."

Michelle sucked in a breath and hoped he was right. Josh kissed the top of her head and murmured that he loved her. And for that moment it was more than enough to make her smile.

"I arranged for a car to meet us with a few of my guards." Akio exited the plane with Josh just behind Michelle. They shielded her, which was silly as, hello, she was a cop for goodness' sake! But it was sweet anyway, and to be honest, it made her feel better given what had happened to Allie.

A very large male raised a hand in greeting.

Akio waved back. "That's Dave Warden, Tracy's cousin and Grace's personal guard."

"Why's he here then? Are things that bad?"

"Good question. I just asked for guards. I assume Dave would only leave Grace if the situation merited it."

Josh's body tightened and he got even closer to Michelle.

"Hey, get in." Dave opened the door and indicated they climb up into the clearly armored SUV. He grinned at Michelle. "Introductions in a moment, let's get out of the open."

Akio had Josh go first and then Michelle, Akio bracketed her other side, and Dave got in the front seat, ordering the driver to get moving.

Dave turned around once they cleared the airfield. "I'm Dave Warden. I'm sorry for lack of a proper introduction back there, I just wanted you safe right away."

He held a hand out and she took it, his totally dwarfing hers. Josh growled low in his throat, and Akio narrowed his eyes at Dave as well. She sighed and looked to Akio, befuddled.

"Really? You do it too?"

Dave laughed.

"I'm Michelle Slattery. Mind filling us in on what's happening so they'll ease back a little?"

"It's what mated wolves do. It's all right, I get it. There's been a fair bit of chatter in the Other community about that scene in Portland. What happened to the witch."

"The witch was my best friend. She has a name. Allie."

Josh squeezed her hand. "He didn't mean offense."

"No, I apologize. I was told she was your friend, and if it had happened to anyone I knew and cared about, I'd be upset if anyone referred to her like that as well. So gossip about how Allie was found is all over the place, as is talk about you coming out here. Jack called from Seattle where he and Lex, the Alpha of the Cascadia Werewolf Pack, had talked. They wanted extra people on you. Better safe than sorry. Especially after the trouble the local witches here have had with mages."

He explained that Jack's mate Renee and her sister had been targeted by some turned witches and mages. Mages with ties to some human separatist groups who'd been working with the disgruntled brother of one of the local ruling members of the jaguar jamboree.

Michelle shook her head. "I can't understand any of this. Why anyone would do that. I understand addiction. God knows I've seen my share of junkies. But a shifter working with human-only bigots? To turn over family to those who'd kill them? What is the world coming to?"

"I wish I knew, Michelle." Dave looked to Josh. "They're putting a big dinner together at the pack house. I'm sure you guys are hungry. Grace wanted me to extend an invitation to stay there if you wanted. They have plenty of room."

Akio shook his head. "They're staying with me."

"Okay. Good idea. Your place is locked up tight."

Discussion went on all around her as she leaned her head back against the seat and listened, her eyes closed. A wall of exhaustion hit her, though she'd been feeling all right after she'd slept on the plane.

Everything swamped her, leaving her overwhelmed and angry at herself for allowing it. There wasn't any other thing to do but exactly what she was doing.

She tried to manage it all. Because what else could she do? Allie sure as hell deserved better than a best friend who was reeling and out of sorts all while she was overjoyed and in love and at turns filled with so much grief she choked on it.

She wanted to sleep for a week. To sleep and sleep and when she woke up she wanted everything to have stopped being so painful and complicated. She just wanted to be with Josh and she wanted Allie back and for all this weird stuff to not be happening.

But she rode across town in an armored SUV with werewolves. Two of which she'd had sex with. One she was bonded to and could feel his emotions like waves.

"I know," Josh murmured. "I wish things could be calmer too."

She opened her eyes and looked into his. He wanted to comfort her. To make her feel better, and just the thought of that made everything else better. She smiled softly and he kissed her.

"We deal with the hand we're dealt. And who am I to complain? At least I can complain. At least I'm alive and I have you and a future that, while filled with strange stuff, is also filled with wonderful new friends and a community of people more like me than not. I just have to—"

The rest of her sentence was cut off as their SUV was hit from the side at a very high rate of speed, sending it up into the air and then off the road and into the concrete walls that separated the road they were on from the highway.

Her ears started ringing and blood got in her eye as she took stock, trying to wipe her face to get her vision back.

"Michelle! Are you all right?" Josh shouted this as he got her out of her seatbelt.

She shook herself a little to clear her head. "I'm alive. Are you okay? Akio?"

A growl as Akio, in wolf form, scrambled into her lap, teeth bared, ready to tear anything that tried to hurt her into a thousand bloody pieces.

"We need to get out. You carrying?" Dave asked from the front seat.

Josh nodded and then spoke. "Yes." He turned his attention to Michelle. "You stay here. Let me go first. We need to take care of whoever it is that hit us."

"You need all the backup you can get," she replied, grateful she'd brought her weapon as she flicked the safety off. "I've had it with all this bullshit. I'm about ready to blow some motherfucking heads off," she muttered, and Josh barked a surprised laugh.

"Only you could make me laugh at a time like this. Keep your pretty ass down."

"I've called the pack, they're on the way with backup." Dave kicked his door open, and she got low, her weapon in her hand. Akio leapt over her, snarling, his wolf protecting her flank.

The car that had rammed them sat a few feet away, the front crumpled, smoke and steam rising from the engine as stinky fluids leaked from the undercarriage.

It was after midnight so thankfully there wasn't a lot of other traffic, but soon enough looky lous would start to gawk from the highway on the other side of the divider. To the opposite side were several blocks of industry, so they wouldn't have to deal with civilians coming out of their homes.

"No one is in the other vehicle. Stinks of stolen magic though. Of rotten meat."

"That's them." Michelle used her othersight and caught the greasy stain of the mages who'd harmed Allie. She caught Josh's attention and jerked her head toward where she saw their energy signatures.

"Stay back."

"No."

She had been about to argue further when she heard automatic-weapon fire and started to dive for cover. Only she hit the ground because her legs just didn't work.

All around her wolves snarled. White teeth, claws. From the ground, she watched Josh's face as he took her in. Watched, amazed, as grief crossed over his features, replaced by rage the type she'd rarely ever seen on anyone's face. And then he was wolf.

Pain pelted her like hail. Bright, hot drops, like knives as she looked down at her hands. Blood. A lot.

Someone, somewhere nearby had latched onto her magick and was tugging it from her. It slipped through her fingers a lot like the blood.

Feebly she fought back. Trying to scream out to Josh, to Akio, to anyone. But nothing came out but the magick and blood pouring from her, and with it, her life.

She was going to die. Jesus, after all the last ten days had thrown into her life, she was going to die on the fucking street across the country from her home.

But she'd be damned if she was going to make it easy. She let down her inner shielding and pulled all the magick she could from around her. She didn't know how to work blood magick, but she called on it anyway. Her control was wild, not focused, but blood was life and life was its own sort of magick and she'd spilled plenty of it there on the street so she grabbed it and she used it, sending pain and hate and rage down the spell siphoning her life away, and she knew it had hit its target when the searing pain lessened to the dull roar of bleeding out on the street and organ failure.

"Josh! Stand down. Goddamnit, stand down." Dave. Yes it was Dave who was ordering him to stop killing the mage who'd shot his mate. The wolf didn't care for Dave's orders and went back to the ripping and tearing of flesh, the taste of blood.

"We have to get her to Grace."

Dave picked the wolf up and got right in his face, screaming at him, shaking him. The man roused and fought his way to the surface, shifting hard and fast, and the grief nearly swallowed him.

"She's not dead yet, but she's close. We have to get her to Grace. Pick her up and get her in the car."

Josh saw her there on the pavement in a pool of blood. She was pale as parchment, and he rushed over with a cry. He picked her up and felt her presence through the link, but it was so very faint.

One of the wolves who had shown up while they fought the mages drove up and opened the door to the car.

"Go! I'll clean up here. Save her life, damn it."

"Why didn't you take her already? Why not the hospital?"

Akio jumped in and growled until Josh snapped out of it and slid in beside him.

The car screamed off into the night, weaving around bodies and the cars that had been wrecked.

Akio shifted back and moved to them, putting his arms around Josh and Michelle both. He kissed her forehead and looked up to Josh. "Dave didn't touch her himself because he was afraid of how you'd react if you smelled her on him. And no hospital can help her. She's been too..."

That made sense.

He didn't know what to do.

"Give me your shirt so we can stanch some of the worst wounds," Josh called out to the wolf in the passenger seat. He and Akio were naked after the shift.

They raced through the streets as the wolf driving called the pack house and spoke through the speakers to Grace Warden.

"We're about three minutes out."

"We'll have the gates open, pull right up to the sliding glass doors and bring her into my office. I've set up a triage table. Hold on, Michelle," Grace called out. "Talk to her, Josh and Akio. Keep her with us."

Josh leaned down to her ear. "You can't die. I won't let you so don't even try. I hadn't realized how much it had hurt to lose you the first time. You're my mate. My life. Don't leave me, Michelle. You and I have a future to live. We have future babies to raise and a wedding to plan."

Akio brushed his fingertips across her forehead and spoke to her in the other ear as well, the fingers of his other hand tangled with Josh's as he did.

"Don't leave me alone," Josh repeated, tears in his voice. "We just found each other again. We were supposed to. I know it. I know you were meant to be in my life and I was meant for yours. I was born to love you, Michelle. I can't imagine a world without you in it, busting my chops. Making me laugh. Loving me. No one has ever loved me like you do."

They arrived, and the doors of what he remembered as Grace's office were yanked open. Instead of yelling and panic, the wolves that streamed out were calm and in charge, and it helped him to carry her at a run—as gently as he could under the circumstances—into the house, following directions as they were given to him.

"On the table." Grace Warden was a petite woman, but a powerful wolf. She gave the order and he complied immediately. "Step back. You don't have to leave the room but I need space to work."

Akio joined him, standing close enough that they touched shoulders. Touch was always important to shifters. Add to it that as their anchor, Akio was in many ways bound to him and Michelle as well, and Josh was glad as hell Akio was there to keep him from losing his shit. He wanted to pace but all his energy was focused on keeping the wolf leashed. The wolf didn't give a fuck about staying calm, the wolf wanted to protect his mate.

He gave in and began to pace in the very small corner they waited in. Two steps. Turn. Two steps. Turn.

Quietly she gave orders to the wolves assisting her as she cut Michelle's clothes off. Someone put an oxygen mask on Michelle, who was so very still Josh's breath caught.

"Even as a witch, she's not...she's been shot more than a dozen times across her abdomen and chest." Grace didn't turn to face him as she spoke. She continued to work on Michelle.

Their bond got thinner and thinner, and he knew in his gut that Michelle was going to die and that could not happen.

Dimly, he noted that Dave had positioned himself close enough to take Josh down should he lose his shit when Michelle died.

"You're telling me she's dying." His voice was flat.

Grace turned to him, her face grave. "Yes. Unless..."

"Damn it, Josh. Now! It has to be now." Akio squeezed his shoulder hard enough for it to hurt.

"I haven't even asked her!" But even as he said it, he knew it didn't matter if she hated him forever for changing her without talking to her first. At least she'd be alive for it.

Cade approached him slowly, his palms showing. Josh's wolf uneasily prowled just beneath the human skin. Josh went very still, breathing in to assure himself that Michelle still lived and that the male standing there was his Alpha as much as Tracy, Nick and Gabe were.

"I'd be honored to do the change, Josh. But it has to be now."

He blew out a breath, and Akio put his arms around him and held Josh tight, burying his face in Josh's neck. "Do it."

Josh hugged Akio back and looked to Cade. Nodding.

"Do it while I get these bullets out. I don't want her healing with anything inside her that I'll have to remove later." Grace didn't look up as she worked. "Josh, she's going to live and be strong, and she's only going to know you made the choice that saved her life."

"Even if she's mad, she'll be alive," Josh muttered.

"Yes. Listen, we had to change Ben over when he nearly died. He's got forever with my sister Tegan because of that. He doesn't regret it one bit."

Cade got rid of his clothes and shifted so fast it left Josh blinking. The more power a wolf had, the faster he could shift.

"I'm done," Grace told Cade and then she turned to Josh. "Hold her hand. Talk to her. She needs to hear you."

He'd been bitten and turned a decade ago. It wasn't by choice and he'd been unconscious for most of it, so he didn't really know what to expect. His wolf pushed into the forefront and took over, allowing the man to keep his skin.

He put his face in her neck and breathed her in. "Beautiful, I'm here. I'm here and I'm not going anywhere. Hold on and fight. When you wake up you'll be stronger and faster. You'll be a wolf, and if you're mad about that, you can't do anything unless you survive. So if you want to kick my ass you have to live to do it. You hear me? Don't you let go. Stay with me, Michelle."

Cade snarled and bit. Michelle cried out and arched, trying to get away, even though she barely held on to her life.

Josh knew tears ran down his face, but he held on to her hand and kept talking to her. Urging her to fight and embrace the wolf racing through her veins. The wolf that would save her life.

Chapter Fifteen

She awoke from dreams of the forest. Of running. Of pain, quicksilver, burning through her like fire.

She remembered dying. Of the way she'd lost more of her anchor to her body as her essence and magick bled from her. And Josh's voice. His hands on her and his voice urging her to fight. Telling her he loved her.

She heard her heartbeat. Smelled blood and pain and...Josh. Other Weres too. Other types of magick.

Teeth. She gasped, choking on her spit at the memory of teeth, and began to cough, expecting there to be pain.

Hands on her and a voice. A female voice and then Josh. That gave her strength to open her eyes. "Why is a woman here?"

The words, as they left her body, had a life of their own. She couldn't quite grasp the thoughts but everything was different.

Josh's face swam into focus. "There you are, beautiful." His smile wavered at the edges. He was pale, but he smelled good. He smelled *hers*. Had she been able to smell him like this before?

"Who's the dish?"

The female in the room laughed and stepped into Michelle's vision. Inside her, an irrational anger stirred that such a pretty woman stood so near Josh. She pushed it back and nearly puked when a growl came from her lips.

Michelle knew she blushed as heat blasted her neck and cheeks.

"I'm wildly flattered. I don't think I've been thought of as a dish in years. Maybe never. I'm Grace Warden. I'm Supreme Alpha here in North America. I'm also a doctor. Is it all right if I check you over? Take your vitals and the like?"

"Yes, sure. What happened?"

"Can I keep her hand while you do?" Josh asked, his voice rusty.

She squeezed the hand in hers. "Better not let go." She croaked this out and realized how thirsty she was. When she got the energy to speak again, she'd ask for water.

"Never." He brushed a kiss against her knuckles. Knuckles covered in dried blood.

Grace efficiently moved, measuring, doing her doctor thing as Michelle struggled to stay awake.

"You're doing better than the last time I checked you." Grace smiled down, brushing the hair from Michelle's forehead. "I'm going to tell you that you were shot sixteen times. Your kidneys were both destroyed, three shots to your lungs, your intestines had multiple holes. You lost so much blood I'm quite frankly shocked you were still alive when they got you here to me. The only explanation is that you're a badass bitch, as my sister-in-law Nina would say."

Grace held a glass of water with a straw to Josh, who brought it to Michelle's lips, and she drank greedily.

"Take it easy or you're going to throw it back up."

She might have been exhausted and weak and woozy, but her brain wasn't broken. And she knew with all that damage, it had to be two months later, which wasn't true as Josh wore the same clothes and was still covered in blood. Her blood. It was hours later, not weeks or days.

"Want to tell me why I'm still breathing after all that damage?"

Grace stood back, and Josh got closer, brushing his lips over hers, over her eyelids, rubbing his face against her cheek and things that had knotted up inside seemed to ease. She responded to him with a rumbled sigh, and she knew right then, before he said anything.

"You were going to die." This man of hers who kept his control even when things got very bad, who protected her and soothed her, lost it then as tears ran down his cheeks. "I couldn't lose you."

"I'm like you now."

He nodded and then shrugged. "Yes. No. Not quite. You're better. I mean, aside from being shot sixteen times. Cade is the one who bit you. I'm strong, but if I'd bit you, you'd have been out a few days. It's only been seven hours. You're a strong wolf. A *live* one. I know you're angry we didn't ask you first. I apologize—"

"Hush! Did you really think I'd be mad that you saved my life? Am I that high strung and difficult then?"

He paused, his look of anguish softening to humor and affection. "Yeah? Well you're beautiful and really good with a gun so I guess you can afford to be difficult. Occasionally. It's just that I never brought it up to you much less asked, and your life is…well, utterly changed."

"I'm alive. To be with you. To find Allie's killers. I'm. *Alive.* Thank you." And really considering the last ten days or so, being alive as a wolf fell into the plus category.

Grace smiled and thumped Josh on the head with a folder. "See? I told you." She smiled down at Michelle. "They were all so worried, and I said you seemed a practical sort and would prefer a life with Josh and vengeance for what these monsters did to your friend to death over a silly thing like being so near death you couldn't be consulted about being turned."

"I'd laugh but I might vomit if I do."

"By all means, you're free not to do that. Josh has been waiting to move you until you woke up, but he's going to take you to one of our guest rooms so you can sleep. You're going to need it to let your wolf get acclimated. You've done a lot in the last week. Mated, anchored, turned. Your wolf needs as much rest and time with the human as the human needs the same."

Michelle had a million questions, but she was so tired she couldn't think. But she did need to tell them about what she'd seen at that house back in Portland.

"Have to tell you what I saw. We rushed here for a reason."

Grace looked to Josh, who sighed heavily. "I told you," he said.

"What?"

"Stubborn." But he smiled when he said it.

"I'll make you a deal." Grace nodded at Josh, who bent and picked Michelle up. "Let him get you cleaned up. You'll feel better after that. Then Cade and I will come up once you're settled in bed and you can tell him then. And, I hope you don't mind, but one of the de La Vegas wants to hear what's going on too."

Josh growled, and Grace winked at Michelle before she addressed Josh. "This one is Renee, she's Jack's mate and a witch. I think she's going to bring her sister Kendra, who is the female Alpha of the jaguar jamboree. She's also a witch who took on a cat so she's eager to meet you. You'll like her, and we can avoid all this silly boy stuff you guys do anytime another male gets near your mate."

"What about me? I wanted to scratch your eyes out earlier when you stood near Josh."

Josh made a grumbly sound that vibrated through her, and she stiffened when she realized the wolf inside her moved. Like, actually moved.

He carried her up some stairs as Grace followed. "It's all right. You get used to the wolf inside. She'll help you. But she'll rise when I'm near. My wolf always does when you're around." Josh kept his voice calm and quiet, and she couldn't help but snuggle into him.

"I think we might be able to have Josh sitting with you when they come in. You'll be possessive, that's how it works, but it should be fine." Grace opened a door to a lovely guest bedroom. "There's a bathroom through there. Akio brought your bag so you have clothes to change into. Get cleaned up. I'll be back to check on you in a few minutes."

She was already mainly naked as he sat her gently down while he turned the shower on before helping her out of the gown thing she'd been wearing.

His hands shook and she leaned out to take one in her own. "I'm here."

He fell to his knees and buried his face in her lap. "Christ. You nearly weren't. You nearly died. You don't...I can't...I've never in my life felt worse. Thank you for being alive and okay. Thank you for not being mad."

She tipped his chin up. "Only you could manage to look gorgeous with smudges of blood all over you. Are you all right? I'm sorry, I should have protected *you*, it's my job too, after all."

He stood, pulling his clothes off and tossing them in a corner. That second consciousness inside her belly perked up as pride rushed through her. He was all hers. This beautiful, masculine, powerful male.

"In." He pointed at the shower. Though all that sternness fell away when he put a hand at the small of her back and helped her in carefully. "I'm fine. I killed a few mages, but not all of them. But I will. There's nowhere on this planet they can hide from me."

"So some of them got away?"

"I'll handle it all. So just stand there and look beautiful and let me do the work."

"Are you mad at me?" she asked, her voice sleepy as he got her hair nice and wet. One of his arms was banded around her waist, helping her stand. Her legs were rubbery, and she kept going very hot and then very cold.

He gently soaped her hair. "Why would I be mad? I'm...I'm fucked up ten ways right now because you nearly died and I have this driving need to run with you. To grab you and run and never look back because I can't bear the thought of actually losing you. I came close enough. People want to kill you and my wolf is really not down with that. And you have a wolf too. And my wolf finds that really, really hot."

He shook again as he babbled, struggling to keep control. The talking helped keep the man in charge.

Her voice softened as she gave over to the way he touched her. "The bond is different now. More intense and I wasn't sure that was possible. You're feeling some really powerful stuff."

He tried to remain clinical as he soaped the blood off her skin.

"I can't believe I don't even have open wounds." She passed her fingertips over the pinked skin where she'd already healed so much.

"Just be glad it's better. A few hours ago it was much worse."

She hugged him, staying snuggled into his body even as his cock got so hard he felt he should probably apologize.

"You saved my life, Josh."

"Cade did."

"No, Cade turned me. You saved my life." He realized she meant something more than just the gunshots, and tears flooded him again. She was the best thing in the world. The finest gift he'd ever been given.

"Um," he tried to speak when she moved, slick from the soap, and her skin slid against his cock and he arched. "Sorry. You just..."

She tipped her head back. "Good to know I've still got it. We can take care of that, you know, before the room fills up with shifters."

"You were shot sixteen times. I can wait to fuck you until you've had some time to recover. I'm a werewolf, not an animal."

"Only you could make me laugh a sentence after you mention how many times I was shot."

Through their link he felt her wave of dizziness, and he got her rinsed off while he held her up.

"Plenty of time for fucking when you're recovered." He turned the water off and helped her out, drying her off carefully, and then he assisted in getting her into soft yoga pants and a shirt.

"Come on, into bed with you, and I'll let people know you're ready. You'll tell them what you saw and you'll rest and that's an order."

"An order?"

"Yes. Don't push me right now, Michelle. I'm on the edge. My wolf is not happy at all that anyone will be coming in here when you're weak."

"You're here to protect me." She said it so matter of fact that he knew she simply accepted it as fact. And that eased some of his anguish.

She continued. "Is everyone okay? I can't believe I didn't ask. Akio? Dave?"

"Ed, the wolf who was driving, was shot twice. He dove to knock you down as I was doing the same. But we were both too late. Akio is fine. He went off to eat because Cade ordered him to. He hadn't left your side since we brought you in." Thank God for his friend and their anchor. He might have lost it without Akio's support.

He pulled the blankets back and helped her into bed before he went to the door and let the wolf just outside know Michelle was ready to talk.

Josh moved back to the bed and grabbed a chair.

"No."

He looked up at her. "No, what, beautiful?"

"I need you to sit here with me. Please. I need..."

He understood and settled next to her on the bed. "You need to be touched. And I get it. I need to touch you so that works out just fine. Shifters, the whole lot of us, we find a great deal of comfort in touching and being touched. You're on the mend and newly changed so you'll need it more."

She snuggled into his side, sucking in a breath. He sucked in his own gasp when she licked his neck.

"You taste so good. Even better now." Her lips brushed over his skin as she spoke and sent shivers through him. "Wow, I can feel your arousal. I mean, here." She squeezed his cock. "But through the bond too. It's...wow. So wow."

He smiled. "When you're ready for it, I'm going to fuck the hell out of you. Just sayin'."

Her arousal twined around his through the bond, and he had to put a pillow over his lap before everyone came in.

Akio entered the room first and moved right to them. He approached the side Josh was on, knowing how possessive and on edge he would be after his mate nearly died. Even with an anchor.

"Hey, little witch." Akio kissed her forehead. "You're looking a far sight better than you were an hour ago. Don't fucking try to die again or I will kick your ass." And then he settled in the chair Josh was going to sit in.

Grace came in next with a tray she handed to Josh. "Eat. There's a mug of soup there for you, Michelle. If you feel up to it, just sip it here and there."

Cade followed and smiled at Michelle. "There she is, my newest wolf. Welcome, Michelle. And congratulations on the bond with Josh."

"Thank you." Michelle cleared her throat. Josh knew how tired she was getting but she'd soldier through. "And I understand you're the one who turned me to save my life, so thank you for that too."

"Some years ago, a short while after Grace and I were mated, she was shot and seriously injured. Of course my very stubborn mate refused to change into her wolf before she knew my sister, who had been critically wounded, was all right. I know, first hand, what it feels like, that sick, helpless nausea as you watch the person you love more than life itself on the verge of death. So it was my honor to make sure Josh didn't have to face the rest of his life without you at his side. And now you're one of mine too."

He sat at the foot of the bed in a chair Dave brought in.

"I'm going to ask Kendra and Renee to come in now, all right? Then you can tell us all what you saw at once and after that, get some rest." Grace posed it like a question, but Michelle heard the steel in her tone. This was a woman used to being obeyed.

And really, sleeping in Josh's arms was going to be her reward so she'd make it through.

Immediately, when the two witches came into the room, the wolf inside her seemed to press against her insides. Josh took her hand and squeezed it. "Drink some of that soup."

She did, and the concentration it took to pick up the mug, sip it slowly and put it back helped her focus on something other than the fact that two beautiful women had just entered the space with her mate.

"I don't even know how you get through every day feeling like this," she muttered.

"You'll get used to it. Things are very strong between you and Josh now. Your bond is new and you nearly died. Your wolf is establishing herself, and she and your human will have to find an equilibrium. It'll come in time and then things will be easier. I promise." Grace patted her foot.

Both witches smiled at her. "I'm Renee. Jack Meyers is one of my mates. He told me about you. Spoke very highly of you as it happens. He's hard to impress so you must be pretty awesome." Renee kept her eyes on Michelle, not quite ignoring Josh, but it was enough to ease her wolf back.

"I'm Kendra. I'm Max de La Vega's wife and the other Alpha of the de La Vega Jamboree here in Boston. I'm also a witch who took on an animal. So after you're recovered, we should talk about that. How it works for me and stuff. Also, I don't know any other witch who is also a shifter so we have so much to talk about."

"Tell us what you saw." Cade sat back in his chair.

Chapter Sixteen

She woke up with a start and remembered. Everything. Being shot. Nearly dying. Josh's voice as she drifted farther and farther away. She was so sure she'd die even as she held on by her fingernails. And then teeth. The fire of the virus as her wolf raced through her veins.

And then telling a room full of shifters about the magic at the murder scene. The way she'd scented wolves in the energy. About the unbearable *wrongness* of the presence she'd felt in that circle.

She'd repeated it over the phone to Lark Jaansen as well. The witch had told her to rest and not worry, that they were on the trail of the mages and Allie's death would be avenged. She also urged Michelle to consider working for Owen as a hunter in Portland, perhaps as a liaison with the wolves there.

It was worth considering. And it was good to have some options when she wasn't sure what she'd end up doing since she would no longer be a cop in Roseburg.

Josh stirred, opening his eyes and looking straight into her heart. She drew in a breath but it was full of his scent, and she went hot and hard and wet with such force it had her swallowing and reaching for some control.

So very slowly, he leaned in until he brushed his lips against her jaw. "My beautiful wolf."

"Hold that thought." She levered from the bed, thinking her legs would still be weak like they were the last time she managed to stand. But they weren't. In fact she felt pretty amazing all things considered. So she brushed her teeth, washed her face and took care of her business before she went back out to him, where he was also getting back between the sheets.

"Now, you should rest." He tried to tuck her into his body but she squirmed to face him, kissing him square on the mouth.

"How long was I out?"

"About ten hours. It's been two days since we landed in Boston."

"Did *you* rest?"

"Yes. Not the whole time. Once you're on the mend you won't need to sleep more than four hours or so a night. I do like a nap during the day though." He waggled his brows.

"Then neither of us needs to rest right now. I feel awesome. And really horny. I haven't had werewolf sex yet. Um, not that I want to as a wolf, cause, well I'm not ready for that. But you know what I mean."

He laughed, kissing her slow and sweet. "It can all wait. You'll need to shift at some point. It's a full moon in two days. The first shift is easiest then. Though with Cade here and being as powerful as he is and your maker, he might be able to—"

She shut Josh up by kissing him again while she struggled out of her pants and panties.

"I don't want to wait."

"You nearly died less than two days ago, damn it."

She rolled over on top of him, moving to straddle his waist to pin him there while she whipped off her shirt. He hissed, his gaze roving over her body.

"I did almost die. I can remember it. Remember what it felt like as my life drained through my fingers like sand. I nearly lost you. Lost this." She undulated herself against his cock. "I got a second chance. Well, I suppose you were my second chance, being alive? After being shot sixteen times? Well that's some miracle stuff right there, and I can't see any reason not to get you inside me right now. I want to live my life to the absolute fullest. One, because you're my man and you look the way you do and you have some very important and impressive skills in bed, but also? Because Allie didn't get a second chance. How can I not live every single moment, if for no other reason than I know most people don't get that extra chance?"

"I don't want to hurt you. You don't understand."

She pulled his shirt off and ran her hands all over the warmth of his skin.

"Don't understand what?" She bent to lick over a nipple, and he moaned, gripping her shoulders. She pushed back, the thrill of that restraint sliding through her.

"If I hurt you I couldn't live with myself. I want you so much I'm having trouble not shaking with it."

She sat up and looked into his eyes. "If I can walk away after being shot, I can handle your cock."

He rolled his eyes but allowed his hands to slide down her shoulders to her arms and hands. "You sure you're all right?"

"Not if you won't satisfy me sexually." She pouted until he took her breasts into his hands, squeezing her nipples between his fingers.

"Look at me."

His gaze flicked from her nipples to her face. "No. I mean my body. The gunshot wounds are barely even pink now. My muscles aren't even sore. I'm better than fine. Better than all right."

"Are you unsatisfied then?" His gaze went hooded and it sent a thrill through her.

"Huh?" It was hard to think with his hands on her.

"You demanded I satisfy you sexually."

"Oh that. Well get to it and I won't be."

He reached down and got rid of his pants—naturally he wore no underwear—and rolled his hips, sliding his cock through her pussy until she writhed.

"Thing is, I don't think you're ready yet."

Gently, but quickly and with more practiced power than when she'd done it, he reversed their positions, and she was on her back as he loomed over her.

"I'm *totally* ready. I promise."

He smiled at her with his predator smile, and it sent a shiver of delight through her. "Maybe *I* need to make you even more ready because I like to."

He kissed her neck and she arched into his touch. "Okay then. That's all right with me."

He kissed his way down her throat, giving her the edge of his teeth and it was...different. Hotter. Her breath caught and her skin heated as it slid against his.

"Yes. I can scent you. Your skin warming, your cunt getting wet and soft for me." He licked over her nipple and then bit the side, which seemed to be his favorite place. Shivers rolled through her and inside her, that other consciousness, her wolf, seemed to arch along with her.

His chuckle was wicked. "Now you know what it does when you bite me. When you mark me and I can see your mark on me the next day."

Michelle raked her nails down his back and reveled in his hiss of pleasure/pain. She wanted to mark him in a way she couldn't articulate. It was fun before, but now? Now she was driven to do it.

She reared up and bit his left biceps, high up, the meat of his muscle between her teeth. He snarled, but instead of pulling away, he pressed into her teeth, which hardened her nipples.

This werewolf sex thing was working out pretty well so far, she had to say. "Yes, just like that, beautiful. Goddamn, you're so fucking sexy." His hands caressed every part of her he could reach as he licked and bit her nipples until she grabbed his shoulders and shoved him down.

"More!"

His laughter brushed against the skin of her belly and then her thighs. He spread her wide and licked, slow and gentle at first until she began to melt into the bed. Then he hummed, sending the vibrations through her clit, making her arch her back on a gasp.

"There we go."

"I'm totally ready," she managed to wheeze out.

"Nope." He did something with his tongue that made her see little white lights.

"Nope what?" Okay so she might have wailed that last bit.

He laughed, the dog. Or the wolf. Whatever. He was purposely teasing her.

"Are you going to make me beg?"

He looked up, over the line of her body, gaze locked on hers as he licked slow and then fast and then slow again. "Maybe. Are you too proud to beg, Michelle?"

She shook her head. "No. Nope. Nope. I'm begging you. Please, please, please make me come."

"I like that." He continued that slow torture, and she pounded the mattress and jerked at how strong she was. He laughed again. "I should have warned you. You're a lot stronger now."

"Get back to work!"

He totally did. This time his pressure was harder, his licks faster as he slid one finger and then another up into her, turning his wrist until he found a spot so unbearably sweet inside her that she nearly jumped up off the bed.

And then he sucked her clit between his lips and let go. And again. And one more time until her pleasure burst through her, filling her up so there was nothing but sensation and her orgasm racing through her veins.

"Just so you know, I'm absolutely sexually satisfied," she mumbled, opening her eyes as he moved to kiss her. She wrapped her arms around him.

"I aim to please."

"You get a gold star. If I could move I'd do a little cheer."

He gave her such a grin. "Yeah? Well my birthday is coming up."

"I can't possibly get my ass in my old stuff, but as it happens the internet loves a slutty cheerleader costume so I'm sure I can get a replacement. Been a while since I've bounced knowing you watched me cheer."

"Best part of my Friday nights, I gotta say." Then he did some fancy-pants move and slid into her in one hard thrust.

"Damn, you are all about the sex moves. It's a good thing I stuck around to benefit from your skills. However, I was going to suck your cock and you got in the way of that."

"Beautiful, there will always be another opportunity for you to suck my dick. Right now I want to be in you."

When he was dirty like that it turned her insides all gooey.

Her hands on his back caught the tension in his muscles. "Let go. You're holding back."

"I shouldn't be doing this at all! You nearly died, damn it, woman!"

"But I didn't die. You saved me. You brought me here and you made the decisions that saved my life and I am here. Here wrapped around you. Here. So when I tell you to let go, it's not because I'm being a martyr, it's because I am fine and I want it hard."

He sighed and kissed her deeply until she melted into his touch. Then he sped up and she didn't just allow it. She reveled in it. She loved how he looked at her with his wolf shining in his eyes.

He thrust deep and hard like it was the only thing he could do. Like he couldn't resist and she loved it. Loved that he needed her so much.

"I love you," he said, leaning his forehead to hers. "Don't leave me. Do you understand?"

She nodded. "I love you too."

When he came he pressed inside, his fingertips digging into her hips hard to hold her still.

She drifted off that way, safe in his arms. Loved.

Chapter Seventeen

Ten days later...

Josh watched as she came back, Tracy at her side. His chocolate wolf, he liked to call his mate, approached and stretched as she took her human skin again. He handed her a sweater, which she put on before getting back into her panties, jeans and shoes and socks.

Tracy and Pam had been teaching Michelle to track as a wolf, and she'd been using her unique talent with magick to attempt to locate the mages. They'd hit many dead-ends but something very bad had appeared on the horizon.

The witches were keeping it close to the vest, but something they called the Magister was responsible for the disappearances. Only they didn't know how to stop it yet. Or even what it truly was aside from a whispered nightmare from legends older than recorded history.

The wolves had upped their patrols, and everyone in a pack, jamboree or pride checked in at least twice a day with their leadership. Michelle had been working with the witches and Pacific to liaise between and keep everyone in Portland prepared.

Back in Boston, they spoke to Akio nearly daily about what was happening as the wolves at National worked with the cats and one of the very few witch clans on the Eastern seaboard.

Big, bad things hung over them, and there was a weight in the air as they did what they could to prepare, but knew it would be bad when it finally came down.

Michelle had clicked with the pack when she'd come back newly turned. Tracy had taken her under her wing as she now shared Josh's rank.

Even better was just how adept she was at the job. Her training as a police officer had prepared her, and she had a natural gift for investigation and most definitely protection.

Plus it enabled them to work together, which meant he got to keep an eye on her. And that they could sneak off here and there to run home and get down.

As if she knew what he was thinking about, she looked up from where she'd been poring over a map with Pam and caught his gaze with a smile.

He'd nearly lost her. It was so close he still woke up in a cold sweat some nights just remembering it. But she was stronger now that she had a wolf. Faster. Better able to protect and defend herself.

It had brought them closer, even as he still had trouble letting her out of his sight for very long. She got that and did what she could to stay in sight or close by. She hadn't been home, though she and her mother had spoken—briefly—on the phone. They'd had a wake for Allie just a few days earlier, and he'd gone with her to Roseburg where they'd packed up her apartment and moved all the rest of her belongings up to Portland.

She checked in on Kathy daily, but she was forging a new life, one with Josh at her side. It wasn't always safe, but she was loved and she filled his life in a way he'd never thought possible.

So when the shit finally hit the proverbial fan, when this Magister thing everyone spoke about in hushed voices finally made its move, he'd protect her with everything he had and they'd survive because there was no other choice.

About the Author

To learn more about Lauren Dane, please visit www.laurendane.com. Send an email to Lauren at laurendane@laurendane.com or find her at Twitter @LaurenDane.

A whole world exists...beneath the skin.

Beneath the Skin
© *2012 Lauren Dane*
de La Vegas Cats, Book 3

Gibson de La Vega is the Bringer, one of the Alpha's right-hand cats. It is his job to mete out justice and defend the law that holds their jamboree together.

After a contentious meeting with another jamboree, he's shot—Mia stumbles onto the scene and saves his life. He's immediately drawn to the female who dug three silver bullets from his body. Even after he discovers she's a Porter, a family his own harmed grievously half a century before.

Mia has enough in her life. She's recovering from a vicious hate crime—an attack using silver has affected her ability to do what she loves most. The last thing she needs is a bossy alpha cat like Gibson. A de La Vega no less.

Despite the myriad reasons to stay away, even as they continue to hunt down the would-be killers, their attraction deepens into something else entirely.

The answers they find bring that threat far closer to home than anyone could have imagined and it'll be up to Gibson to end the mess once and for all. And up to Mia to stand at his side, even as he risks his life...

Warning: A super hot alpha male with a gruff façade, and an uppity female who's not buying it. Some violence. Some red-hot sex. Bad words. Lots of fun.

Available now in ebook and print from Samhain Publishing.

She can't shift, but she can shake their world.

Diamond Dust
© 2013 Vivian Arend
Takhini Wolves, Book 3

Caroline Bradley is having one hell of a week. Her wolf lover has sniffed out his mate, making her an instant free agent. Not only that, Takhini territory has been overrun with aggressive bear-shifters electing a clan leader, and the wolf pack is feeling the effects—pushing her diplomatic skills to the limit.

Tyler Harrison is a grizzly on a mission. If he's going to win the majority of the bears' votes, he needs one final thing: a female companion. The only woman in town with influence over wolves, humans, and more bears than he'd like to admit, is Caroline.

Despite the sexual pull between them, though, Tyler's not seeking a permanent relationship. And Caroline isn't looking to be anyone else's political pawn. But she should have remembered that when shifters are involved, changes happen in the blink of an eye.

Warning: Billionaire bear hero plus kick-ass human heroine equals a sexually volatile power struggle. Get ready for what might be the naughtiest game of tag that's ever been played in the great outdoors.

Available now in ebook and print from Samhain Publishing.

It's all about the story...

Romance

HORROR

www.samhainpublishing.com

CPSIA information can be obtained
at www.ICGtesting.com
Printed in the USA
FFOW04n1546131214
9410FF

9 781619 219625